"Why did you ask me out here today?"

"Because I like you," he said simply. "And because when I'm with you, all I can think about is kissing you."

Her stomach did a flip. Her heart fluttered. The sun seemed even brighter and the sky even bluer.

"Say something," he muttered. "If you want me to get back on my horse and forget this conversation ever happened."

"Do you kiss with your hat on or off?"

With his hands still holding hers, he smiled. "No one's ever asked me that before."

"It's nice to be first at something," she joked.

"Raina, you are the most intriguing woman I have come across in years. And to kiss you, I'm definitely taking my hat off." When he leaned in closer to her, she closed her eyes.

But his mouth didn't cover hers. Instead, she felt his lips touch whisper-soft, slightly above her ear.

"A kiss shouldn't be too quick."

Dear Reader,

I'll always remember the first time my husband and I really talked. In sharing, we connected on a deep level, inspiring trust that has lasted through the years. To form that bond, we had to become vulnerable to each other.

My hero, Shep McGraw, is a strong, silent Texan. A marriage of convenience teaches him he must lower his guard to trust his new wife. By risking vulnerability, he discovers the love and understanding that can lead to happily ever after.

I hope you enjoy Shep's transformation from guarded single dad to my heroine Raina's white knight. Shep and Raina's romance is Book 5 in my THE BABY EXPERTS series. I hope readers will look forward to Book 6 in the series, coming in December 2010.

Readers can learn more about THE BABY EXPERTS at www.karenrosesmith.com.

All my best,

Karen Rose Smith

THE TEXAN'S
HAPPILY-EVER-AFTER

KAREN ROSE SMITH

Silhouette®
SPECIAL EDITION®
Published by Silhouette Books
America's Publisher of Contemporary Romance

SILHOUETTE BOOKS

PLEASE RECYCLE
THIS PRODUCT IS RECYCLABLE

ISBN-13: 978-0-373-65526-7

Recycling programs
for this product may
not exist in your area.

THE TEXAN'S HAPPILY-EVER-AFTER

Visit Silhouette Books at www.eHarlequin.com

Printed in U.S.A.

Books by Karen Rose Smith

KAREN ROSE SMITH

Award-winning and bestselling author Karen Rose Smith has seen more than sixty-five novels published since 1992. She grew up in Pennsylvania's Susquehanna Valley and still lives a stone's throw away with her husband—who was her college sweetheart—and their two cats. She especially enjoys researching and visiting the West and Southwest where her latest series of books is set. Readers can receive updates on Karen's releases and write to her through her Web site at www.karenrosesmith.com or at P.O. Box 1545, Hanover, PA 17331.

To Sis and Bern, our son's godparents.
Thanks for the difference you made in his life.
Happy birthday, Sis. Bern, we miss you.

Author's Note

Adoption procedures may vary according to state,
individual circumstances and agencies.

Chapter One

Shep McGraw hurried to the emergency-room door. In his arms, two-year-old Manuel let out a cry that echoed in the hospital's parking lot.

Tension and worry tightened Shep's chest. He'd been through this before with Manuel's earaches. Thank goodness Dr. Raina Gibson, the boy's ear, nose and throat specialist, had been on call for her practice tonight. He thought about his two other sons, who were with their nanny. They hadn't liked him leaving this late at night.

As Shep rushed through the automatic glass doors, he remembered another fateful E.R. visit many, many years ago. He shoved that out of his mind and hugged Manuel closer.

The woman in charge at the registration desk looked him over—from his tan Stetson to his fine leather boots—and he had to rein in his frustration with red tape. "My name's Shep McGraw. I'm meeting Dr. Gibson here to treat my…son."

"Mr. McGraw, if you'll have a seat—"

Manuel's crying had tapered off slightly, but now he screwed up his cute little round face and howled loud enough to scare his black wavy hair into disarray.

Shep shifted Manuel to his shoulder. "My boy needs someone to look at him *now*." He was about to add that the Lubbock hospital had all of his information on file, when Dr. Gibson came through a side door and crossed to the desk.

Although Manuel's crying still rent the waiting area, the beautiful doctor's appearance impacted Shep as it always did. Her Native American heritage was attractively obvious in the angles of her cheekbones and chin. Tonight she'd pulled her long black hair back into a low ponytail and clasped it with a beaded barrette. The white coat she wore molded to her long legs as she hurried toward him.

She greeted the woman at the desk as she reached for Manuel. "I'll take him back, Flo."

After patting Manuel's back and making soothing noises that quieted him, she said to Shep, "Give Flo your insurance card so she can put through the paperwork." Then she headed for the door leading to the examination cubicles, motioning him to follow.

Shep took out his insurance card, slapped it onto the desk and followed Raina. He couldn't help but admire her graceful stride, the straightness of her shoulders, even as she held Manuel and headed for the exam room. He had to smile at the sneakers she wore that made her look more like a runner than a doctor.

All was quiet for the moment in this part of the E.R. wing. Manuel's cries had faded to tiny hiccups. Shep felt so sad sometimes for this little boy, who'd been neglected, taken away from his mother and put in a foster home. Shep knew all about foster homes firsthand, though there was no indication the couple who'd cared for Manuel was anything like the foster parents Shep had lived with.

At the door to the exam room, Dr. Gibson paused and waited for Shep to precede her inside. Although Shep considered himself more cowboy than gentleman, he motioned her to go ahead of him. With a small smile and a quick nod, she did. But when she passed him, he caught the scent of lemon and his stomach twisted into a knot, as it did whenever he got too close to her. He didn't get too close to her if he could help it—for lots of very good reasons.

Raina glanced at Shep as she settled Manuel on the gurney. "On the phone you told me this started about an hour ago?"

"Yes. Before I put him in his crib. At first I thought he was just overtired or didn't want to go to bed. But then he started pulling on his ear, so I took his temperature and saw he had a fever."

"I'll take it again," she assured him with quiet efficiency. Her gaze met his. The earth seemed to shake a little and they both quickly looked away.

With coiled energy wound tight inside him, Shep moved to the gurney to hold Manuel. He hadn't intended it, but somehow his hands got tangled up with hers before she pulled them away from the little boy. Their gazes connected again…and this time held. Shep's blood rushed fast, and in that instant, he thought he saw returned interest in the pretty doctor's very dark brown eyes.

A moment later, he guessed he was mistaken. In a small town like Sagebrush, Texas, where they both lived—about fifteen minutes from Lubbock, where this hospital was located—certain people had a higher gossip profile than others. Dr. Gibson was one of them.

He'd asked his nanny, Eva, if she knew any particulars about the doctor, and he still remembered what Eva had said. "Her husband was a firefighter in New York City. He died saving others on September eleventh. Somehow, she picked up her life and finished her schooling, then returned here to be with her family. I can only imagine what she's gone through, and it's not something I ever want to even *think* about going through."

As Shep studied Raina Gibson now, he saw no signs of a tragic past—unless it had carved those tiny lines under her eyes and fostered the ever-present quiet and calm he sensed about her.

She went to the counter, where she took an ear thermometer from its holder. When she returned to the table, she focused solely on Manuel. "This little guy has been through so much. I feel so sorry for him. Another ear infection is the last thing he needs." She cut Shep a sideways glance. "Or *you* need. How are Joey and Roy?" She had treated eight-year-old Joey last year for a sinus infection that wouldn't quit.

"They're good. They get upset when Manuel's sick, though. Roy's afraid he'll lose more of his hearing."

Raina studied Manuel's temperature and frowned. "It's one hundred one." Seconds later she was examining the toddler with the otoscope and then her stethoscope. Finally, she gave Shep her verdict. "I don't like the looks of this, Mr. McGraw."

"Shep," he corrected her, not for the first time. After all, Manuel had seen her at least three times over the past six months.

Now she didn't avoid his gaze, but looked him directly in the eyes. That was his first clue he wasn't going to like what she had to say.

"Okay, Shep."

That was the second clue. He had the feeling she'd used his first name to soften the blow.

"I'll give you a prescription again for Manuel, to get this cleared up. But I have to recommend that you let me do a procedure to put tubes in his ears. I'm afraid if we don't, he'll lose his hearing altogether."

Before he caught himself, Shep swore. "Sorry," he mumbled. "I just don't want to put him through anything else." He picked up his son from the table, easily lifted him to his shoulder where Manuel snuggled against his collarbone.

Raina's gaze was sympathetic, her voice gentle. "I know what he's dealt with already. But he's in your care now, and I can see that you love him. You have to think beyond the procedure to when he's three or four. You have to do what's best for him long-term."

Shep patted Manuel's back. Finally, he said, "Tell me what's involved."

Taking a few steps closer, Raina stopped within arm's reach. "The surgery's called a myringotomy. I make a tiny incision in the eardrum and any fluid will be removed. Then I'll insert a tympanostomy tube into the drum to keep the middle ear aerated. We'll leave the tubes in from six months to several years."

She was close enough that Shep was aware of her body heat as well as his. "Will he have to have surgery to remove them again?"

Tilting her head, she ran her hand over Manuel's hair then brought her gaze back to Shep. "No. Eventually they'll extrude from the eardrum and fall into the ear canal. I'll be able to remove them during a routine office visit, or they'll just fall out of his ears."

Shep could hardly imagine his small son in this big hospital, with medical personnel caring for him. "And you believe we have to do this?"

"Shep, Manuel has already lost some hearing. You know that from the assessment I did. I'm afraid if we don't do this, he'll have speech problems, too."

"And the downside?"

"I'll give you a sheet of information and you can read about the pros and cons. As often as you're bringing Manuel to me, I don't think you have a choice."

"I hate hearing statements like that," Shep muttered.

Manuel began crying again and Shep rocked him back and forth. "How long will this operation take?" he asked over the baby's heartbreaking distress.

Raina leaned closer to him, as if in empathy…as if she might want to take Manuel into her arms again…as if she hated seeing a child cry.

"Ten to fifteen minutes. It's done on an outpatient basis. Manuel will be given anesthesia. Once he's recovered from that, he can go home. Chances are good he'll feel better right away, because that pressure in his ears will be released. He's been suffering with this for too long. And so have you," she added with an understanding Shep found almost unsettling.

Again, their gazes locked and neither of them seemed to be able to look away. Shep didn't know what was happening to him, but he didn't like it. Every time he stared into those impossibly dark eyes of hers he felt unnerved, and if he was forced to admit it, aroused. That wasn't what he should feel, standing in this cubicle with her while he held Manuel. He should feel grateful...nothing else.

He must have been scowling from here into the next county, and she misinterpreted his expression. "I know you're worried. Every parent worries when anything is wrong with his child. But try to anticipate a positive outcome. Think about Manuel *not* having any more painful earaches."

"The anesthesia bothers me," he admitted.

"You must trust the doctors here. Give us a chance to help him."

Shep was used to being in control. His history had taught him not to let anyone else run his life...let alone his son's. "How soon do you want to do this?"

"How about next week?"

"That soon?"

"You have a housekeeper, right?"

Did she remember this kind of information about all of her patients? "Yes, Eva. She'll be able to take care of Joey and Roy if I'm not home."

Obviously thinking that distracting him for a minute might be a good thing, Raina said, "Roy's and Joey's adoptions are final now, aren't they?"

"Yes, they are."

"And Manuel's?"

"I'll be his dad in a few months, if all goes well."

"I admire what you're doing, Mr. McGraw."

"Shep," he reminded her again, suspecting she used his surname to distance herself. Why would she need to distance herself? Could she be as interested in him as he was in her? It had been a long time since he'd wanted to pursue a woman....

"Shep," she repeated, her cheeks coloring a little. "Giving these boys a home is so important. And you obviously care about them a great deal."

"I wouldn't have decided to adopt them if I didn't. The foster-care system—" He shook his head. "It's not like it once was, but it's hard for children to feel loved when they don't know where they'll be sleeping the next night."

After being abandoned by his mother, a series of foster homes, as well as a chief of police, had convinced Shep he wasn't worthy of anyone's love…until a kind rancher named Matt Forester had proven differently. Matt had been Shep's role model and he was determined to give Roy, Joey and Manuel the same leg up in life that Matt had given him and his friend Cruz.

Raina was looking at him thoughtfully, as if there were more to him than she'd ever realized. Her intense gaze made his interest in her reach a new level, and he had to tamp down a sudden urge to touch her face.

He felt warm and uncomfortable, and now just wanted to get the prescription for Manuel and leave.

The doctor cut through the awkwardness between them by suddenly pulling a pamphlet from a stack on the counter and a pad from her pocket. She wrote out the prescription, then handed the papers to him. "Go home and think about the procedure. Look at the pamphlet I've given you. I'll be in my office tomorrow. Call me if you have any questions."

Someone knocked on the door.

Raina went to it and opened it, then returned with a few papers. "You need to sign these before you leave."

As he signed the forms, he tried to make conversation—anything to distract himself from her quiet beauty. "Did you come in just for Manuel, or have you been here all day?"

She gave a shrug. "This has been an exceptionally long day. I had office hours this morning, surgeries this afternoon and a complication that kept me here." At his look, she was quick to assure him, "Not for anyone who had tubes inserted in their ears."

Shep smiled the first smile that had come naturally since he'd entered the emergency room. "You knew I was going to ask."

"You're the type who would."

"Type?"

"You *care,* Mr. McGraw. You ask questions and you want answers. That's a good type to be when you're a parent." There was admiration in her voice.

"You're going to have to practice using my given name."

Another blush stained her cheeks. "Maybe I will. I'll walk you out."

As they strode side-by-side to the reception area once more, Manuel stilled on Shep's shoulder. He could tell the little boy was almost falling asleep. His crying had exhausted him.

Raina must have seen that, because as they stopped

at the entrance to the hallway leading to the pharmacy, she peered around Shep's shoulder at Manuel's face, and then gently patted him on the back. "I imagine he'll get more sleep tonight than you will."

"You probably imagine right."

Standing there like that, staring down into her eyes, Shep felt totally unsettled. His gut tightened, his collar felt tight and he was overcome by a desire to kiss her.

He was absolutely *crazy.*

A woman like Raina Greystone Gibson wouldn't give a man like him a second look. Her husband had been a hero.

And Shep?

He was no hero…and because of his past, he never would be.

The following Wednesday, Raina hurried to the day-surgery waiting room. Manuel had been her last surgery of the day, and she was eager to bring his father good news. However, when she reached the doorway to the waiting room she stopped cold as her gaze went immediately to an obviously nervous Shep McGraw.

To her dismay, she felt flustered, knowing she was going to have to talk to him again. That was ridiculous! She didn't fluster easily. But something about this tall, lean cowboy got to her, and she couldn't figure out why. Since Clark had died, no man had made her feel much of anything. But then, the way Clark had died probably had something to do with that.

Closing her mind to memories she didn't revisit often, she watched Shep McGraw for a few seconds. He sat alone, away from the others in the waiting room, staring at the cable-channel news on the TV. But she could tell he wasn't really absorbing what he was watching. He'd checked his watch twice since she'd stood in the doorway.

Why did he get to her? Because he was such a concerned dad? Shep had had such a difficult time stepping away from Manuel to let the baby be taken to surgery. Still, she'd seen concerned fathers before. Maybe he got to her because he was a single dad doing the best he could with the boys he was adopting?

That had to be it. After all, she knew Manuel's story because Shep had given her the baby's history the first time she'd treated him. Manuel had gone into foster care malnourished and sickly when he was almost seventeen months old. A month after that, Shep had received a call from a contact working in the system who'd told him about the boy, asked if he was interested in adopting a third child. Shep had gone to see Manuel and made the decision on the spot. Thank goodness the toddler's mother had finally cared enough to sign away her parental rights. Manuel's father was nowhere to be found.

Raina suspected some particular motivation drove Shep to save children from the system. She was becoming more and more curious as to what that motivation could be. Not for the first time, Raina reminded herself her interest couldn't have anything to do with Shep's six-foot height, dark brown hair, the very blue eyes that reminded her of a Texas sky on a clear summer day. He could probably crook his finger at a multitude of women and they'd come running. But he wasn't crooking his finger, and she wondered why.

She'd heard he was well off. He'd bought a huge

ranch on the outskirts of Sagebrush, invested in a barnful of horses, remodeled the house and refurbished the barn. He'd also purchased a business—a lumberyard. He might look like a cowboy on the outside, but inside she got the feeling he was a shrewd businessman. He'd supposedly made a bundle selling commercial real estate in California before moving to Sagebrush. Yet he didn't flaunt his wealth. In fact, the locals said he spent a good bit of time at the lumberyard as well as working his ranch.

He glanced at the doorway. Spotting her, he was on his feet in an instant.

She stepped a few paces to the side of the doorway for a little privacy, faced him and smiled. "Manuel came through the procedure with flying colors. He's in recovery. If you'd like to come sit by his bed while he wakes up, that's fine. After he's aware that you're there, we'll wait another half hour or so until the anesthesia wears off. Then you can take him home."

"Just a half hour? Are you sure he'll be okay? And you said something about instruction sheets and eardrops."

Impulsively, she reached out and clasped his arm. "Shep, he'll be fine. We won't let you leave without the instruction sheets."

As her fingers made contact with his tanned skin, sensations registered from her fingertips to her brain—his heat, the strength of the muscle in his forearm, the tingling in her belly that seemed to come from nowhere. His eyes met hers, and for a moment they were both aware of the contact. She quickly released his arm.

He was wearing a Stetson, and he took it off now and

ran his hand through his hair, ruffling it. "Will you take me to him?"

"Sure."

They walked side by side down the hall. Shep was six inches taller than she was—a couple of inches taller than Clark. But where Clark had been husky, Shep was lean. Clark had worked out with weights to keep his body in prime condition for his job. But she had the feeling Shep McGraw's muscles came from his work on the ranch and at his lumberyard.

She shook her head to clear it from such insane thoughts. "Will your housekeeper be available this evening?"

Shep arched a brow at Raina.

"I just wondered if she'll be helping to care for Manuel tonight."

"More than likely she'll keep Roy and Joey busy so that I can take care of Manuel. Eva often jokes that I moved from laid-back California to Wild West Texas never expecting life to be as unpredictable as it has been. But I don't regret one day of it and I don't think she does, either. I'll show her anything you show me, in case she needs to know."

"Is she…older?" Raina asked, telling herself she needed the information for purely professional reasons.

"Don't let *her* hear you say she's older," he joked, with a wry smile. It was a crooked smile that made Raina's pulse beat just a little faster. "She's in her fifties," he went on, "but won't say exactly *where* in her fifties."

Raina chuckled. "She sounds like a woman after my own heart. We should never have to divulge our age."

"Let me guess," Shep said. "You're thirty-seven."

"How did you—?"

"Gotcha," he teased. "I have a friend who's a doc in Santa Fe. I know how long med school took him. And you started practicing here after your residency, right?"

"A year and a half ago," she confirmed with a nod.

"That's about when Joey and Roy came to live with me."

"And Manuel joined you six months ago."

"That's right. It's been a roller-coaster ride."

She laughed. "You're a brave man, Shep McGraw, taking in three boys and having the confidence to raise them."

"Confidence or insanity," he muttered.

She laughed again.

They reached a door with big black letters—Authorized Admittance Only. Raina opened the door and let Shep inside. He spotted Manuel right away and made a beeline for him, Raina hurrying to catch up. She glanced at the monitors, then asked the nurse at Manuel's side, "How's he doing?"

"He's doing great."

Shep caught a stray stool with the toe of his boot and dragged it to Manuel's bedside. He sank down on it and took the little boy's hand. "How are you doing, kiddo? There's nothing to worry about now. I'm here and we're going home soon."

"Home?" Manuel repeated, his eyes still a little unfocused.

"Yep, home. Joey and Roy and Eva are waiting for us."

Raina went to a side counter, picking up a sheaf of papers. She brought them over to Shep, then went over the instructions for giving Manuel the eardrops, as well as changing the cotton in his ears. "Everything's explained here. If he runs a fever or if anything seems out of the ordinary, call me immediately. My service can page me."

Shep's attention shifted from her to his son in the bed. His gaze ran over Manuel—from the little gown he was wearing to the cotton in his ears.

Shep was quiet for a moment, then he swiveled around on the stool to face her. "Are you done here for the day?"

"Yes, I'm off to run some errands. But as I said, my service can always contact me."

"How would you like to do something a little more exciting than running errands?"

"And what would that be?" She was really curious.

"How would you like to come to the Red Creek Ranch and get a taste of just how wild the West can be?"

Chapter Two

Raina was stunned by Shep's invitation.

"Why do you want me to come to the ranch?"

For a moment, he looked as if he was going to clam up, pull down the brim of his Stetson and walk away. But then he gave a small shrug, stood, lodged his hands in his back pockets and studied her. "You're a no-nonsense kind of woman, aren't you?"

"Does that require an answer?"

"No," he drawled, with a lazy Texas slowness that made her stomach jump. Then he became more serious. "After what you've been through, I imagine you don't have time for crap. Life's short, and you know it."

No one had ever approached the subject of her widowhood quite like this before. She was even more intrigued by this man who had been getting under her skin a little every time he had an office visit with one of his kids. "That's one way of putting it," she admitted wryly.

Sliding his hands out of his pockets, he dropped them to his sides. "The truth is…" He hesitated and then said, "I like you and I trust you. Manuel had an operation and anesthesia. The hospital is sending him home just an hour afterward. That doesn't sit comfortably with me. On top of that, I need to do some things, like the drops and all, and I don't want to make a mistake. I'll be glad to pay for your time. I'm not asking you to do this for free."

He *liked* her. She decided not to focus on that. "So you'd consider this a house call?" If she looked at this in professional terms—

"Yeah, sort of. Maybe a little longer than a house call. After all, it's going to be suppertime soon. You could stay and eat with us."

There was nothing obvious in the way Shep was looking at her, and yet…she was very aware he was a well-built man. From those silver sparks in his blue eyes, she had the feeling he appreciated who she was, white lab coat and all. This was the oddest situation she'd ever found herself in. Over the past nine years, she hadn't taken a second look at a man, and had always put up a shield or run quickly if one looked interested. Why wasn't she running now?

Because this was mainly about Manuel, she told herself.

"I don't usually make house calls."

"Is it on your list of things you never wanted to do, or on your list of things you just never have done?"

In spite of herself, she had to laugh. Shep's sense of humor was one of his charms. Raina thought about the

Victorian where she lived. It would be empty tonight. She'd missed Gina Rigoletti the day she'd moved out to live with her fiancé at his estate. Gina's sister, Angie, had moved in with her last week. But as a pediatric nurse, she was working the night shift. And her friend Lily was away in Oklahoma with her recently deceased husband's family. Her husband had been killed in Afghanistan while serving his country.

Raina suddenly realized that at one time she'd craved solitude, but that wasn't the case now. After Clark died, her grief had gotten held up by everything surrounding September eleventh—the immensity of everyone's loss, the days of horrible nightmares, the government settlement. She'd watched way too much TV, unable to tear herself away from it, hoping to learn more...to see Clark's face *somewhere*. Grief had finally overtaken her the day she'd gone to Ground Zero, seen all the pictures posted and been overwhelmed with the realization that the man she loved was never coming home. Now, nine years later, she felt as if she'd finally found herself again. Returning to Sagebrush, being near her family, had helped her do that.

So here she was, with this rugged single dad asking her to his ranch. "Basically, you want my help with Manuel?" she asked Shep directly.

"Yes. I'll pay you outright. Insurance won't be involved."

"You could hire a nurse, though I really don't think you need one."

"First of all, I don't want a nurse. I want *you*." The way he said it seemed to disconcert him a little. The muscle in his jaw jumped. But he went on anyway. "And secondly, I have two other boys to think about. They're going to be worried about Manuel. I want to make sure they don't have anything to be afraid of by the time they go to bed tonight."

Making a sudden decision—from sheer instinct—Raina said, "No need to pay me. Let me tell my house-mate where I'll be. She's working upstairs. Then I'll come home with you for a little while, just to see how things are going."

After an automatic last check of Manuel's monitors, a look into his adorable dark brown eyes, Raina left the recovery room, wondering what in the heck she was doing.

As Raina's hybrid followed Shep's shiny new blue crew-cab truck down the gravel lane, she thought about how absolutely different she was from the rancher. The types of vehicles they drove were only the tip of the iceberg. So why was she following him to his ranch as if...

As if she were attracted to the man?

She was here for Manuel's sake. That was the beginning and the end of it. Though she *was* curious how a single rancher managed to handle two rambunctious boys and a baby. Wasn't it part of her duty as a doctor to find out?

The beautifully maintained split-rail fencing lined the lane. Pecan trees and live oaks kept the road in shade. To the left she spotted horses, at least ten or twelve, and a new-looking lean-to that could shelter them from the weather. When she drove a little farther, she caught sight of a huge red barn with Red Creek Ranch painted in shiny black letters above the hayloft doors. On the right stood a spacious two-and-a-half-story ranch house that looked as if it had been recently refurbished with tan siding and dark brown shutters. The wide, white wraparound porch appeared to be an addition to the original structure. A swing hung from its ceiling. She caught sight of curtains fluttering at the windows and was surprised to find herself thinking the house looked like a home.

To the left of the house, set back, a three-bay garage stood waiting. Shep headed for the parking area in front and she followed, her tires crunching on the stones as she parked beside him. Then she went to the back of his truck to help him with Manuel. The little boy was awake, but not altogether himself.

"He's usually yelling and screaming to be let out of his car seat by now."

"Give him some time to get back to normal."

As Shep reached for Manuel, the two-year-old began to cry. "What did I do?" Shep asked worriedly.

"Are you grumpy after you have a tooth drilled?"

"Sometimes," Shep answered warily.

"Well, think about how Manuel must feel."

To Shep's surprise, when he held Manuel in the crook of his arm and closed the back door of the truck, the little boy reached toward Raina.

"Do you think she can do a better job of making you feel better?" Shep asked, half serious, half joking.

Manuel stared at his dad for a few seconds, then reached for Raina again.

Shep shrugged. "Go ahead."

"This has nothing to do with your ability to take care of him," Raina assured him as she cuddled Manuel close and let the baby lay his head against her hair.

"There's a basic difference between men and women," Shep decided. "That's what this is all about."

"And that difference is?" Raina asked, not sure she wanted to know.

"Women are softer. Men are harder. It's a matter of comfort."

Raina couldn't help but hide a smile as she followed Shep up the porch steps to the front door and into the house.

A ceiling fan hummed in the large living room and tempered the noise coming from beyond. Raina caught a glimpse of a colorful sofa, its covering stamped with rodeo cowboys and horses. Black wrought-iron lamps and comfortable-looking side chairs complemented the casual decor. Sand art on the wall appeared to be hand-crafted, as did the mandala over the sofa and the blue pottery painted with gray wolves high on the bookcase. The big flat-screen TV was a focal point in the room.

Manuel tucked his face into her neck and she snuggled him closer. She liked the feel of a baby in her arms. Once she'd hoped a child would be a possibility. But so many possibilities had died on September eleventh, along with her husband.

At first, she'd thought about him twenty-four hours a day, seven days a week. Memories still popped up now and then without her summoning them. But time was taking its toll, and life went on, whether she grieved and remembered or not. Life had swept her along with it, and she'd stopped resisting its force, though a deep ache was always there.

As they neared the kitchen, loud boys' chatter turned into more of a shouting match. Six-year-old Roy and eight-year-old Joey were coloring at a large rectangular pedestal table. But Joey was now drawing on Roy's picture, and in retaliation Roy was drawing on Joey's.

They were pointing fingers and making accusations while a woman in her fifties, with white-blond spiked hair and long dangling earrings stirred a pot on the stove and firmly called their names. "Roy. Joey. Stop squabbling. You don't want your dad to come in and hear you."

"Dad's too busy to hear us," Joey said defiantly, his dark brown eyes snapping in his mocha-skinned face.

Roy nudged his brother's shoulder. "Dad don't want us to fight."

"We're not fighting," Joey declared, making another mark on Roy's paper. "We're just drawing."

"Drawing very loudly," Shep admonished them as he stepped through the doorway into the kitchen. "Eva, shouldn't they be helping you get supper ready?"

"We did help her," they both chimed in unison, running to him for a hug.

"Oh, I just bet you did."

Suddenly Joey looked around Shep and saw Raina. "What are *you* doing here? Did she come to do something to Manuel or to me or Roy?"

Raina couldn't imagine what they thought she'd do. She'd examined Joey when he had a sinus infection, but that had been about the extent of it.

"Why is she carrying Manuel?" Joey wanted to know.

Raina suddenly wondered if any parent could answer all of the questions a child might ask in one day.

"Dr. Gibson came home with me to make sure Manuel feels okay," Shep responded, and quickly introduced her to his housekeeper, who had kind, hazel eyes.

"The doctor came home with you so you can spend time with *us*," Roy decided, looking happy at *that* idea.

From their exchange Raina guessed Manuel's earaches had shifted most of Shep's attention to him, and the older boys didn't like it.

"Supper in fifteen minutes," Eva called. "Boys, you'd better wash up."

Their heads swung to Shep almost in unison, and he nodded. "Do what Eva said."

But before they ran off to the bathroom, Roy studied Raina again. "Are you staying for supper? We're having chili. Eva doesn't make it so hot, 'cause I don't like it that way."

Raina laughed. "I don't know if I'm staying."

"We'd like you to," Shep said quietly.

Eva added, her eyes twinkling, "I made plenty."

She really hadn't intended to stay and share a meal. Sharing a meal formed a…bond. But with little Manuel clinging to her, Roy looking at her hopefully, Joey studying her a little suspiciously and Shep standing only a few feet from her, giving off signals that he wanted her to stay, she agreed. "All right. Thanks for the invitation. My mom makes chili, too, and I don't like it too hot, either."

At that, Roy grinned and ran off with his brother to wash up.

Manuel cuddled against her, looking up at her with big brown eyes. "How do you feel, little one?" she asked gently.

He reached for her chin, and when his fingers made contact he said, "Rocky, rocky."

Raina looked to Shep for an explanation. He was

watching Manuel's fingers on her skin. He was looking at her lips. She felt hot and cold, and much too interested in what Shep was thinking right now.

Eva explained, "When Manuel first came here, all he wanted Shep to do was to rock him in the big rocking chair in the living room."

Raina bought her attention back to Manuel's words. "I suppose he's associated rocking with comfort. I can do that."

"I can hold dinner longer, but the boys are going to get their hands dirty again," Eva warned.

"There's a solution," Shep assured her. "I'll bring the rocker to the table."

"She still won't be able to eat if she's rocking Manuel."

Since Raina would rather talk with than be talked about, she assured them, "I can rock and eat at the same time. It might get a little messy, but maybe I can get Manuel to drink."

Eva nudged Shep's shoulder. "I can see why you brought her along. She's on top of things."

"I'll say she is," Shep said, looking at her almost as if he didn't *want* to be looking at her. The same way she knew she shouldn't be looking at him?

Dinner was a rowdy meal, as the boys dipped corn bread into their chili and talked with their mouths full. Roy told Raina about his bus ride that morning and afternoon. Joey talked, mostly about Roy—but not about himself.

After supper, the boys helped Eva clean off the table and Raina was impressed. "I could never get my brother to do that unless I bribed him."

"Your brother's the police officer, right?" Shep asked.

"Don't tell him I told you about the bribing. I'll never live it down."

"Rumor has it he's a good detective."

She knew small towns listened to the rumor mill more than cable news channels.

Thoughts of Sagebrush's gossip line faded as Manuel stirred. She brought her head down to his and whispered close to his ear, "You're such a good little boy."

He looked up at her as if he'd heard every word, and gave her a smile.

Shep was sitting next to her in a high-backed wooden chair that looked like an antique. He leaned closer to her. "Whispering words of wisdom in his ear?"

With Shep's face so close to hers, she became breathless when she gazed at his lips. "Just some positive reinforcement. You can do that for him anytime."

"I'll remember that," Shep returned in a low, husky voice, then leaned away.

To distract herself from the magnetic pull Shep exuded, she complimented Eva on her chili, as well as on the corn bread, the coleslaw and the ginger cookies she'd baked for dessert.

Suddenly Shep stood. "Okay, boys. How about if you go get ready for bed? Morning comes a lot quicker when you have to go to school."

Roy's "Aw, do we have to?" and Joey's quick look at Raina had Shep arching a brow. "I'm going to get Manuel changed into pj's, too. I want you two finished by the time I'm done."

Both boys mumbled, "Yes, sir," slid last peeks at Raina, then scrambled off.

After they were gone, Eva said to Raina, "They find

toys to play with and forget to put their pajamas on. I'll go up and make sure they don't get too sidetracked."

"Thanks," Shep called to her, and Raina could see he meant it.

"I guess it's time to put those eardrops in," Shep said with a frown. "Is there a right way and a wrong way?" he asked Raina.

"If we coax him to lay on his side, that will make it easier."

Shep motioned through the doorway to the living room. "Let's go to the playroom. I set up a changing table in there."

Raina wasn't used to being around a man who put kids first. Gina's fiancé, Logan, did. He'd had to. But Raina didn't know Logan all that well yet.

Shep took Manuel from her, his large hands grazing her midriff as he securely took hold of the little boy. She was surprised by her body's startled awareness of the man's touch. Her cheeks flushed and she felt oddly off-balance.

Shep looked down at her, their gazes locking for a few intense moments. Neither of them said anything as Shep carried Manuel, and Raina followed him to the playroom.

They passed what looked like a guest bedroom, then entered a bright, sunny room with yellow walls. There were two long, floor-to-ceiling windows that looked out over the backyard and smaller ones in a row on the other side.

"Was this once a porch?" she asked.

"Yes, it was. I closed it in, put a smaller porch on this entrance and fenced in the yard."

"Did you do it yourself?" If he did, she was curious

why. He could have hired an entire crew! Now she really
was curious about him.

"A contractor did most of the work on the ranch for
me. I wanted it restored rather than razed and rebuilt.
But I did this. I learned to work with my hands early on.
I like building things. I guess that's why I bought the
lumberyard, so I could help other people do it."

He took Manuel over to a dark wood chest with a
changing table on top. The room had been furnished
with kids in mind—a couple of royal blue beanbag
chairs, a game table with stools, cupboards and
shelves that held toys—everything from remote-
controlled vehicles to drawing sets. This room created
a pang of longing in Raina, a pang she hadn't experienced in a very long time. Clark had wanted children
badly. So had she.

"What are you thinking about?" Shep asked her.

With that question, Raina knew he could be a perceptive man. But she didn't share her private thoughts very
easily. "I was just thinking about parents and kids. When
did you know you wanted to adopt?"

As he undressed Manuel, Shep seemed to consider
her question very carefully. "I knew about foster care
firsthand. I grew up in the system. It wasn't pretty. Once
I got a start in life and learned how to make money, I
had a goal—to find a place I could turn into a real home
for kids, kids who needed a family as much as they
needed a roof over their heads."

Shep set Manuel's shirt aside, but it began to slip
from the table. Raina caught it. Closer to Shep now, she
could almost feel the powerful vibrations emanating
from his tall, hard body. She sensed he was all muscle,

all cowboy, silent much of the time, only revealing himself when he chose or had to.

"Why Sagebrush?" she asked.

"Why *not* Sagebrush?" he responded with a quick grin that she realized he used to disarm anyone who maybe got too close. That grin had the power to make butterflies jump in her stomach. She hadn't felt that sensation for so long she almost didn't recognize it. But when she felt a burning heat crawling up her neck again, she knew exactly what it was. Attraction. She'd been fighting it ever since she'd met Shep McGraw.

Concentrating on their conversation, she took a quick breath. "This isn't an area of Texas most people think about when they want to move somewhere. I just wondered how you landed here."

Shep helped Manuel into a pajama shirt covered with horseshoes. The toddler yawned widely as Shep concentrated on the tiny buttons, his fingers fumbling with them.

"My father came from Sagebrush. He died when I was four. Then my mother and I moved to California. So you might say I just returned to my roots."

Raina knew she should back away from Shep and his story, which was bound to deepen her awareness and sympathy. She didn't want to get involved with *anyone*. She'd lost her husband in the most awful of ways, and the aftermath had been heart-wrenching. Moving on had been an almost insurmountable task. But she *had* gone on. She was past tragedy. And she wanted to keep it that way.

Still, she was *so* intrigued by a cowboy who could run a ranch and a lumberyard, yet change a diaper, too. Trying to be as tactful as she could, she asked, "And you lost your mom, too?"

"Yeah, I did."

When Shep didn't say more, Raina moved a step closer to him. "I'm sorry."

Stilling, he peered down at her. He was so much taller than she was. The blue of his eyes darkened until she felt a tremble up her spine.

"Don't be sorry," he said, his voice husky and low. "Everything that happened to me back then made me who I am now."

Who *was* Shep McGraw, beyond a rancher and a dad? Did she even want to find out? Wasn't that why she had accepted his invitation tonight?

The moment was broken when Manuel began kicking his legs and reached his arms out to Shep. "Up, Daddy, up."

Shep broke eye contact and concentrated on the little boy. "Not yet. Let's get you changed so we can put your eardrops in."

"Dwops?" Manuel repeated.

"I left them on the kitchen counter," Shep told Raina. "Would you mind getting them?"

No, she didn't mind. She felt as if she needed a breather from him and the obvious love he felt for his sons.

A few minutes later Raina distracted Manuel as Shep squeezed in the drops. Both of them seemed to be going out of their way not to get too close, not to let their fingers touch, not to let their eyes meet.

Footsteps suddenly thundered down the stairs. "Dad! Dad!" Roy and Joey called as they ran through the living room towards the playroom.

"I'm right here," he said with a laugh, "not out in the barn."

His gentle rebuke didn't seem to faze the boys. "We want to say good night to Dr. Gibson. Eva said we could."

Raina drank in the sight of the two little boys, her heart lurching again. What was wrong with her tonight? Joey was dressed in pj's decorated with racecars. Roy's were stamped with balls and bats. "I'm glad you came down."

"We're not going to bed yet," Joey explained. "We can read in our room before we go to sleep. Dad says that quiets us down."

Raina couldn't help but smile. "Sometimes I read to quiet *me* down before I go to sleep."

"We wanted to ask you somethin'," Roy volunteered.

Raina glanced at Shep but he just shrugged. "What did you want to ask me?"

"Can you come back and see the horses sometime?"

She didn't know how to respond. What did Shep want? What did *she* want? Did that even matter, when these two precious children were staring up at her with their big, dark eyes? "I suppose I can."

"Promise?" Roy asked, possibly sensing her hesitance.

Joey added, "If you promise, you have to do it. Dad says no one will be your friend if you can't keep a promise."

Again her gaze sought Shep's. His expression was friendly but neutral. Apparently, this was her decision. She liked the idea of him teaching his sons about promises being kept.

"I promise," she said solemnly.

"If you come Saturday, we can go for a ride after we do chores," Joey informed her, as if warming to that idea.

"You can *help* with chores!" Roy added enthusiastically.

At that, Raina laughed out loud. "Well, maybe if I'd help you with chores, I'd develop some muscles. My brother's always telling me I should work out."

"You have a brother?" Roy asked, wide-eyed.

"Sure do." She thought about her schedule Saturday. "I'll tell you what. I have to go to the hospital Saturday morning, but then I'll stop by here afterward." She looked at Shep. "Is that all right?"

"That's fine," he replied, still giving nothing away.

Eva came into the room then, and asked Shep, "Is Manuel ready?"

The two-year-old had cuddled against Shep's shoulder. Now Eva took him and said, "Come on, boys. Let's head on up." As they followed their nanny, they turned around and stared at their dad.

He assured them, "I'll be up in a few minutes. Go on. Pick out a book you want me to read to you." He said to Eva, "I'll bring along some of that oat cereal for Manuel."

After Roy waved at Raina, both boys took off after Eva.

Feeling awkward, Raina checked her watch. "I'd better be going."

"I'll walk you out."

Raina gathered her purse from the counter, feeling Shep's gaze on her as she went to the door and he followed. She wondered what he was thinking. She knew what *she* was thinking.

The end-of-August evening was warm. As they stepped outside, the breeze tossed the ends of her hair. They walked to her car in silence.

The motion-detector light on the side of the house glowed as they neared her car. She knew she was going to have to ask Shep the question in her mind. Distracting herself for the moment, she pressed the remote and her doors unlocked.

Shep opened the driver's-side door for her.

Rather than climbing in, she faced him, close enough to him to see the beard shadow on his face. "Do you want me to come out on Saturday?"

"You have to. You promised."

"I know. I wasn't sure what to say. When Roy looked at me with those big eyes, I didn't know how to refuse."

Shep chuckled. "I know exactly what you mean."

"You didn't answer my question." She needed to know if he wanted her here or not.

"I like you, Dr. Gibson. It won't be a hardship to take you on a trail ride."

"Raina," she said softly. "If we're going on a trail ride, first names seem more…comfortable."

"Comfortable," he agreed, looking down at her with interest she hadn't noticed in a man's eyes for years. He shoved his hands into his pockets, though he didn't step away. "Thanks for coming over tonight."

"I really enjoyed myself."

Awkwardness settled between them, the kind of awkwardness that happened after a first date, she thought. Only, they hadn't been on a date. Still, she felt pulled toward Shep. Yet something else urged her to move away—probably memories, heartache and regrets over a love lost.

After she slid into the driver's seat, Shep closed the door. Then he laid his hand on the open window and bent down, his face close to hers. "Remember, a promise given is a promise that should be kept."

She had the feeling his boys had had promises made to them that weren't kept. He was protective of that and protective of them. "I'll remember," she murmured, unable to take her gaze from his face.

Shep straightened and stepped away from the car.

With a trembling hand, she pressed her smart key to start the engine. As she backed out of the parking space and drove away, his words echoed in her mind.

A promise given is a promise that should be kept.

Did Shep McGraw keep *his* promises?

Chapter Three

"**Y**ou are wrong!" Roy yelled. "Wrong, wrong, wrong."

"I am not," Joey yelled back.

"Boys," came a stern voice.

Raina had parked beside Shep's ranchhouse and, hearing voices at the barn, headed to it. She walked toward the corral, guessing the boys were outside the stall doors. At the fence, she stopped.

Shep had crouched down in front of Roy. His voice wasn't stern now, as he said, "It's still early. Not even lunchtime."

"But she said she'd be here this morning."

Raina had gotten tied up at the hospital and intended to phone on her way to the ranch, but her cell phone had lost its charge.

"Hey, everybody," she called, cheerily now, letting them know she was there. "Am I too late for chores?"

"Dr. Gibson!" Roy cheered, brushing away his tears. "You came." He turned to his brother. "I told you so. I told you she'd keep her promise."

Shep slowly rose from his crouched position. Without any accusation, he said, "The boys were a little worried you'd forgotten."

Opening the corral gate, she stepped inside the working area for the horses. "I'm sorry I'm late. I got tied up at the hospital." She lifted her duffel bag. "I brought old clothes and riding boots."

"You can change at the house or in the tack room," Shep informed her.

"The tack room is fine."

"She's a girl," Joey said with disgust. "She thinks about clothes and getting them dirty."

Raina could see Shep was trying hard to suppress a laugh. He knocked his Stetson higher on his head with his forefinger. "Listen, Joey, part of a woman's job is to think about clothes. You ought to do it once in a while."

As Joey crinkled his nose, Raina laughed and headed for the tack room. A few minutes later, she returned in her old jeans and short-sleeved blouse, her dad's navy paisley kerchief tied around her neck. "Just tell me what you want me to do."

"We saved mucking out the stalls," Roy told her.

"I'm thrilled about that," she responded with a straight face.

He took a good look at her and smiled. "You're teasin'."

She ruffled his hair. "Yes, I am. I guess no one really likes mucking out stalls, but it has to be done."

"You're really going to do it?" Joey asked.

"I did it before, when I was about your age. My uncle had a ranch and a couple of horses."

"In Sagebrush?" Shep asked.

"Yep. On the east side of town. When hard times set in and he had to sell it, a developer bought it. There's a whole bunch of houses there now, where his ranch used to be."

Her gaze met Shep's and one of those trembles danced through her body again. It was like a preliminary tremor to an earthquake. She told herself she was being foolish. She was just off balance, being out of her comfort zone, being with Shep and his boys again.

"We'll get the shovels," Joey told Raina as he and Roy headed into the barn.

After they were out of earshot, Shep asked her, "Did you have second thoughts?" His blue eyes demanded a straight answer, not a polite excuse.

"I did. But I'd made a promise."

"Should I ask why you had second thoughts, or leave it alone?"

"You're direct, aren't you?"

He shrugged. "I try to be. Life is complicated enough, without beating around the proverbial bush."

When she hesitated before answering, he settled his hand on her arm. "It's okay. You don't have to explain."

She'd worn a short-sleeve blouse because of the early September heat. Shep's long, calloused fingers were warm and sensual on her skin. When she looked up at him, she felt tongue-tied. It was an odd experience, because she usually wasn't at a loss for words.

Finally, she admitted, "There are a lot of reasons why I had second thoughts." The awareness between her and Shep wasn't one-sided. She knew that now. She could feel his interest, and she wanted to run from it.

He released her arm and held up one finger. "The first reason is me." He held up a second finger. "The second reason is me." He held up a third finger. "And the third reason is probably me."

"No ego there," she muttered.

He laughed. "It has nothing to do with ego. I just figure— Hell, Raina. I know about your husband. I also know for the past six months you did everything you could not to make eye contact with me."

"Manuel was my patient."

"Yeah, I know that."

"Well, *you* didn't show any interest, either."

"No, I didn't. I pretended there wasn't any, just like you did."

"I wasn't pretending," she protested. "I wasn't interested. I'm *not* interested. I loved my husband, and when I lost him—" She stopped. "I can't ever explain what it was like—waiting and not knowing, waiting and hoping, waiting and waiting and waiting. And finally accepting, and having to deal with grief deeper than I've ever known." She shook her head, struggling to maintain her composure. "I never want to feel anything remotely like it ever again."

"I can understand that."

She saw empathy in Shep's eyes. Real empathy. He'd lost his parents, and she didn't know who else he might have lost along the way. Maybe he knew, too, that nothing was forever…nothing lasted.

"I came because I made a promise," she repeated.

A smile crept across Shep's lips. "Then Roy was right to trust you."

The way Shep said it, she had the feeling *he* didn't trust many people. Because of the way he'd grown up?

"Roy and Joey don't fight often. For a couple of years, all they had was each other."

"For a couple of years?"

"When their parents were killed in an accident, they were put into the system. But being biracial, and being brothers, the system had trouble placing them. So they stayed in foster care."

"Maybe the fact that they're fighting means they don't have to depend on each other quite so much, since they have you."

"I'd like to believe that's true, but they still hold back with me. Especially Joey. He likes to keep things to himself, and sometimes that causes him trouble."

"Do *you* keep things to yourself?"

"Oh, terrific. My boys had to ask a *smart* lady to come to the ranch for a trail ride."

This time *she* laughed. The scent of horses and the sun's heat beating on old wood rode the corral air. Although Shep didn't always say a lot, he was easy to talk to. He made her feel…safe. She'd returned to Sagebrush to feel safe, to be close to her mother and brother, to establish roots that had somehow slipped away on that terrible day in 2001. She'd felt safe in the Victorian with Gina, and now Angie. But not safe in this way. Not protected like this. She suspected Shep was a protector, and that gave her an odd feeling. Clark had been a protector, and because of that he'd died.

"You're thinking sad thoughts."

How could Shep do that? How could he know? "Not for long. As soon as your boys hand me a shovel, I'll only be thinking about getting finished and going on that trail ride."

Shep motioned her inside the barn. "Then let's get started."

The barn was old. Raina could tell that there were signs of it being refurbished—fresh mortar between stones on the walls was lighter gray and without cracks. Some of the wooden stall doors looked new, their catches and hinges shiny and untouched by time.

"How old is the barn?" she asked, realizing the boys were nowhere in sight.

"The buildings on the property date back to the 1850s."

"You bought a piece of history."

"That's the way I look at it. That's why I didn't raze everything to the ground and start over. I liked building on what was here, making the old stand up to the test of time. Do you know what I mean?"

"I do. It's nice to know something will last with a little help." As she took in the stalls and the feed barrels, she asked, "Where are the boys and their shovels?"

Shep shook his head. "I know where they are. Come on." He led her past the tack room, and when they rounded the corner, she saw Joey and Roy leaning over a pile of hay bales. The hay was stacked wide and high. But the boys were sort of in the middle of it, two bales up, peeking over the edge of one bale.

"Kittens?" she guessed.

Shep nodded, smiling. "You *have* been around barns. They wanted to bring them up to the house, but I told them the babies are still too little. They haven't even learned how to climb out of their nest yet. Give them a few more weeks and they'll probably be sleeping with the boys."

"You sound resigned."

He chuckled. "I know kids can get attached to animals. Pets can give them security, so I'm all for it."

Without thinking twice, Raina climbed up the bale and sat next to Joey. She peered over the edge and saw a mama cat nursing four little ones whose eyes were barely open.

"They know where to go to eat," Roy told her, as if that was important information.

Joey added, "Dad says we shouldn't touch them until they climb out. Their mama wouldn't like it."

"Your dad's probably right. The mama cat might move them and then you wouldn't be able to find them."

"Until they're old enough to run around," Joey said, as if he were challenging her.

"Yep, that's true. But in here they're protected from the weather and anything else that might bother them. So it's a good place."

Joey seemed to think about that. "Yeah. I like the barn. It's even neater when the horses are in here making noises."

"I'll bet," Raina responded, holding back a grin.

"Come on, boys. If we don't get those stalls cleaned out before lunch, you don't go on a trail ride," Shep reminded them.

Without grumbling, they crawled down the bales, rushed into the tack room and emerged with three shovels. Roy handed one of them to Raina. "Dad uses a pitchfork, but he won't let us touch that."

"It's locked in the tool closet," Shep explained. "I'll go get it and meet you at stall one."

Chores went quickly, and Raina noticed Shep did most of the work. He wanted the boys involved, to have a good work ethic, but he wouldn't give them more than they could handle.

By the time they reached the third stall, Roy was slowing down.

Raina said, "Why don't I give you a hand?" She put her shovel aside and stood behind Roy, helping him scoop and carry to the outside bucket.

He grinned up at her. "That was easier."

Joey didn't say a word, but there was no indication he resented his little brother having help when he didn't.

When they'd finished with the third stall, however, Shep suggested, "Let's take a break. Go on up to the house and tell Eva we're ready for lunch. Wash up. We'll be along."

A few minutes later, Raina stood beside Shep, watching the boys race out of the barn through the corral gate and across the lane. "They're hard workers."

"Yeah. And sometimes I think they'll do anything for my approval. That's not always a good thing."

"I don't know what you mean."

"I want them to be themselves. I want them to be who they are with each other when they're in their room alone. When I'm around, they're more guarded."

"They've been with you what—a year and a half?"

"Yep. And you'd think they'd be more comfortable with me by now."

It was easy to see that Shep was the strong, silent type. She wondered how much sharing he did with his boys. How much he told them what he was feeling. But she didn't know him well enough to say that, so instead she said, "There's distance between me and my mom, even now. But my brother and I are really close."

"You don't tell your mother what you're thinking?"

"No."

Shep didn't ask why, and his look told her he wouldn't pry if she didn't want him to. So, instead of keeping her childhood hidden, as she usually did, she brought it out to examine once again. "My father was Cheyenne, and proud of it. He told me and my brother about the old ways of living, of thinking, of believing. My mother didn't like that. She wanted us to fit in. Sometimes being proud of our heritage didn't help us fit in. Ryder and I were often made fun of, but we had each other and I didn't tell her about it. That sort of set the standard for our relationship. I tried to be what she wanted me to be—the perfect daughter. Daddy and I could always talk, but my mom and I couldn't. He died when I was ten, and nothing was ever the same after that."

Shep nodded as if he knew all too well exactly what she meant. "Did your mother work before your dad died?"

"At the library. But afterward, that wasn't nearly enough, so she started driving a school bus, too."

"Gutsy lady."

"I think in her heart she always wanted to be a teacher, but never had the money to go to college. She practically runs the library now. She gave up bus driving a few years ago to take the head position."

"She sounds as interesting as you are."

Raina wasn't sure what to say to that, so she fell back on what had affected her life most deeply. "My mom never got over losing my dad. It was like that part of her, the romantic side of her, just stopped existing."

"Has that happened to you?"

Raina really had not seen the connection before, and

now she did. "I think that's happened to me because of the way Clark died."

"I suppose that's so. Your husband was a hero. His memory is bigger than life, so there's no room to have a romantic dream again."

"How do you understand that so well?"

"I've been around."

Sometimes Shep's attitude was too enigmatic, and she found herself wanting to dig down to deeper levels. So she asked a question that had been niggling at her for a long while. "If you wanted a family so badly, why didn't you get married?"

"Because having a family didn't depend on me marrying."

"That's not an answer," she protested softly, wanting to step closer to him, and yet afraid of feelings that were starting to tickle her heart. So afraid, she wanted to run.

He seemed to have an inside battle with himself, then finally said, "I don't trust women easily. I have good reasons to believe they leave when the going gets tough. Or they stay for the wrong reasons."

"The wrong reasons?"

"Yeah. Things like money. Fancy cars. A house in the best neighborhood in town."

So he'd gotten burned by a woman who had wanted what he could provide for her? Or had the trust issues started much earlier than that?

"Everyone's got baggage, Shep. It's what we do with it that matters."

When he angled toward her, she wasn't sure what was going to happen next. She was a bit surprised when he took hold of a lock of her hair and let it flutter through his fingers. "You're a captivating woman, Raina. Do you know that?"

"No," she said seriously. "Each day that passes I figure out more about myself."

"What did you figure out today?" He let his hand drop and she was sorry when he did.

"I figured out that mucking out a stall is as good an exercise as I can get in a gym. And that little boys always have a next question, even when you think you've answered them all."

He chuckled. "Isn't that the truth?"

He looked as if he wanted to kiss her. To her amazement, she wanted him to do it. But why—so she could feel like a desirable woman once more? So she could really start living again? So she could wipe out some terrible memories and replace them with sparkling new ones?

Whatever the reason, it didn't matter, because Shep took a step back. "We'd better get up to lunch before there isn't any. Those boys have big appetites after doing chores."

Shep had let her down easy. They'd gone back to friendly. His trust issues and her past could be hurdles that might prevent even a meaningful friendship from beginning.

What had gotten into him?

Shep gave his horse a nudge up a small hill, watching his sons in front of him as they did the same. Raina rode between Joey and Roy, talking to them as they bounced along.

Shep rarely discussed his background or his breakup with Belinda. Only with Cruz now and then. Granted, he hadn't given Raina much, but he'd said more than enough. He wanted to forget Belinda's gold-digging motivation for getting engaged to him…the indifference to children she'd kept well-hidden. He needed to forget that kid who'd gone through life without an adult to really care about him. He longed to forget landing in jail at the age of fourteen. He'd never tell Raina Greystone Gibson *that* story.

He'd been so rebellious back then. He'd hated his foster parents and their neglect. Not only of him, but of Cruz, too. Cruz had been younger, more vulnerable, not as experienced as Shep about the ins and outs of the system. Shep had felt he had to look out for him. But in protecting Cruz, he'd broken the law.

No matter their foster parents had left them alone for the weekend. No matter Cruz had taken ill and had a raging fever. No matter Shep hadn't known what to do except hotwire that old truck and take Cruz to the closest E.R.

The chief of police had thrown him into that dirty jail cell and not cared a whit. If it hadn't been for Matt Forester rescuing them, Shep wasn't sure where he or Cruz would be today. Maybe in prison. Maybe on the streets.

Nope. He'd never tell Raina about that chunk of his life. She'd never understand the desperation that had driven him to rebel against authority figures for his sake as well as Cruz's.

He'd sensed that same defiant spirit in Joey and suspected it had developed while he was in foster care.

The brothers had had loving, caring parents until they'd been killed. With no relatives to take care of them, they'd been thrust into the system. Then five,

Joey had acted out, and his aggressive behavior had made placement even harder. They'd been through two foster couples before Shep had decided to take them.

He believed there were three secrets to turning kids around. Matt Forester had taught them to Shep and Cruz. You gave children safety. You gave them love. And you gave them a reason to trust you. If Shep could accomplish that, Joey, Roy and Manuel would be on their way to being confident and finding a future that fit them.

Breaking Shep's consideration of his past and present, Joey turned around and called, "Can we show Dr. Gibson Red Creek?"

"Do you remember how to get there?"

"Yep. We go right at the bottom of this hill."

"Lead the way."

Joey grinned and pushed his fist up into the air, as if he'd just been given a gift. The gift of confidence, Shep hoped, as he urged his horse to catch up to Raina's.

"They're good riders for their age," she remarked as the two boys trotted ahead.

"You're pretty good yourself."

"I must have inherited good riding genes from my ancestors who roamed the plains."

He couldn't tell if she was being serious or tongue-in-cheek. "You said your heritage meant a lot to your dad. Did it mean a lot to you?"

"That's not an easy question."

"Tell me," he said, surprising himself. Usually when conversations with women got into sticky waters, he swam in the opposite direction. But he wanted to know more about Raina, wanted to uncover everything she kept hidden deep in her soul.

"Is it a long way to the creek?" she asked with a wry smile.

"Long enough that if you haven't ridden for a while you're going to be sore tomorrow."

"I guess I'd better soak in a hot tub tonight."

"It wouldn't hurt." He suddenly had visions of her sinking into a tub full of bubbles. But before she slid into those bubbles—

He had to quit imagining her in something less than a blouse and jeans.

When she canvassed his face, he wondered what she saw. He could hide quite a bit with his Stetson. Every cowboy knew how. But they were riding in the sun, and the shadows from his brim didn't hide everything. Could she see his interest in her was physically motivated? Since Belinda's rejection of a future he held dear, all he'd looked for from a woman was physical satisfaction.

He and Raina were so blasted different. The ways were too numerous to count. So why was he here? And why was *she* here?

Curiosity, pure and simple.

She was still studying him when he said, "You changed the subject."

"You helped it along."

"I did. And if you really don't want to talk about it, that's okay."

She was silent as they rode through pockets of wild sage, scrub brush and tall grass. As her horse rocked her, she turned the kerchief around her neck, the frayed edges brushing her skin. "This was my dad's. He wore it whenever he went riding. He liked to tease that it would come in handy if a dust storm came up. His stories about his father serving in World War II, as well as his own experiences in Vietnam, were written down in a diary he kept. My mother gave it to me on my twelfth birthday."

"Why your twelfth?"

"I was having trouble fitting in at school. I didn't know how to handle being Cheyenne, and at times growing up, it made me feel like an outsider. Ryder faced the same problem, but a guy can be a loner and that can be attractive by itself. He knew who he was when he hit his teens. He also knew he wanted to be a cop. I just felt…different from everyone else."

"When did you stop feeling different?"

"I never did. But I learned to *like* being different. Remembering the myths and fables my father told me helped me see how life fit together, how the past becomes the present, how being Cheyenne is something to be proud of. But it wasn't always so, and I feel guilty about that."

"You were a kid."

"Yeah. A kid who should have listened more. Who should have known better. If I had listened to the stories my father told, instead of trying to deny my heritage, my life might have made sense sooner."

"I think you've done one heck of a job with your life."

Raina shook her hand. "Shep, you don't know me."

He reached over, clasped her arm and they both stopped their horses. "Med school isn't a walk in the park. I know you're a fine doctor who cares about her patients. I can see you love kids and should have a bunch of your own."

"Oh, Shep."

He wasn't sure, but he thought her eyes were a little shiny. His hand slid from her arm down to her hand. "What's wrong?"

Then he swore. "That was really a stupid thing to say. And a stupid thing to ask. You're wishing you did have a bunch of kids with your husband. You want the life back that was so brutally taken away from you."

She took a deep breath. "It's been nine years. The first five, that was probably true. The next couple, I tried not to keep looking back, because that only brought anger and sadness and regret. Returning to Sagebrush made a difference for me, and I probably should have done it sooner."

"Getting away from New York?"

"Yes. Stepping away from the memories and starting over."

Shep watched Raina's dark hair blowing in the wind, saw the determination in her eyes to forge a new future. But determination wasn't always enough to push regrets aside.

After a long look at each other, they headed toward the sound of the boys' laughter.

Fifteen minutes later, at the bank of the creek, Shep dismounted and so did Raina, without any help from him. She was definitely an independent woman, one who charted her own course.

He went to help Roy dismount and saw Raina go to Joey. She hadn't asked if she should help. She just saw the need and handled it. But he noticed she waited to see what Joey could do for himself, obviously not wanting to step on the little boy's pride.

She'd make a wonderful mother.

Now, where in the heck had that thought come from?

He and his little band were just fine on their own, although he had to admit, their caseworker seemed to doubt his ability to handle a toddler. But he'd shown her so far that he could, and he had Eva to help with practical matters. He didn't need anyone else.

But as he moved to stand beside Raina, watched the boys walk a little farther down to listen to the bubbling creek, he had to admit he was damn attracted to her. A night in his bed—

He cut off the thought. She wasn't that kind of woman. After the obviously loving marriage she'd had, she'd only look for another committed relationship. If she looked at all.

And to be honest, he couldn't commit to a woman because he didn't trust them.

Cruz had tried to analyze him. More than once his friend had suggested that his trust issues stemmed from his mother abandoning him at a mall when he was six…from his foster mothers not really caring…from Belinda wanting what Shep could give her materially rather than emotionally. Shep didn't know about all that. He just knew it was hard for him to open up to anyone—to trust anyone.

Yet, standing beside Raina, inhaling the lemony fragrance of her that carried to him on the breeze, appreciating the lines of her profile and the soft fullness of her lips, his groin tightened and all he thought about was kissing her.

Her gaze met his and he knew she'd caught him. She didn't play coy games, but said simply, "You were staring. Do I have hay in my hair? A smudge of dirt on my nose?" Her question was light, but he sensed the underlying tension.

"You look like you belong out here, with the horses and the wind, breaking trails and maybe riding shotgun."

She laughed. And he smiled. And then they were leaning a little closer to each other.

"Hey, Dad. Come see the rock I found," Roy called to him.

Saved by the voice of a child, Shep thought as he leaned away from Raina, tapped his Stetson more securely on his head and went to see the treasure his son would be carrying home.

His life was his boys. And he couldn't—wouldn't—forget that.

Chapter Four

"It seems longer than a few weeks since we really talked to her," Raina said on Sunday evening. She stood at Lily Wescott's front door with Gina Rigoletti and her sister, Angie.

They were all worried about Lily. A few months ago, she'd been so happy in her marriage, fulfilled in her work helping women conceive. Then a little over a month ago, she'd become a widow. Shortly after her husband, Troy, had been deployed to Afghanistan, he was killed in action. A shock to them, and Lily had been devastated. She and Troy were only married for a year.

"I know," Gina agreed, pushing her black curls behind her ear. "Phone calls just aren't the same. But she needed to be with Troy's family in Oklahoma."

Angie pushed a lock of dark wavy hair out of her

eyes. "I wasn't sure I should come. After all, I don't know her as well as you two do."

"Lily can use all the friends she can get right now," Raina assured her new housemate. "We'll just have to take our cues from her. But she needs us right now. I've been through this. I know that when the casseroles and the cards and the phone calls stop, sometimes you lose your compass. You don't even know if breakfast comes before lunch."

Gina put her hand on Raina's shoulder. "You've never really talked about how it was for you."

"Did your family stay with you in New York?" Angie asked.

"Mom did. Ryder had to get back here to work, and I understood that. Actually, it was a relief when Mom left and friends stopped coming by at all hours of the day. Don't get me wrong, I appreciated all of it. I don't know what I would have done without the support. But I also needed time alone, just to sit and realize that Clark was never coming back. I imagine that's what Lily's doing now," Raina said, sighing. "Our situations aren't so very different."

"Maybe she can talk to you about it," Angie ventured.

"Maybe. We'll see."

When Gina rang the bell, they all seemed to hold their breath.

A few seconds later Lily opened the door. Her blond hair was pulled back into a tight ponytail and she had purple smudges under her eyes. She gave each of them a hard and long hug, then wiped a few tears from her eyes. "I thought all the tears were gone. I don't know how any can be left."

The front of Lily's apartment was a huge, open space. The kitchen flowed into the dining room, which flowed into the living room, with no barriers except some furniture in between.

Lily went to the kitchen, the rest of them following, then stood there as if she'd lost her purpose. "I'm a mess," she admitted. "After I arrived in Oklahoma, Troy's family didn't leave me alone for a minute, and I appreciated their support. But then last night, when I got in, after I called you, I just…I just couldn't figure out what to do next." Her gaze went to Raina's. "When will I feel like I'm back in my body again? That the world's real and I'll understand Troy isn't going to walk through that door?"

Her eyes filled up and Raina went to her and put her arm around her. "Everyone's different. But little by little you'll find a new normal."

"I can't even *imagine* normal! I go into the garage where Troy had his workshop and see the furniture he'll never finish. I put my hand on my tummy and it seems impossible that he's gone and I'm going to have our baby. A month ago—" She stopped abruptly. "I'm sorry. I'm a put-one-foot-in-front-of-another sort of person. Now I look in the mirror and I don't even know who I am."

Raina took Lily by the arm and pulled her into the living room. They all sat on the long sectional sofa.

Angie said, "I've never gone through anything like this, Lily, but when I have a crisis, work helps. When are you going back?"

"I don't know. I called Mitch last night, too. He understands since he served in Iraq. He said to come in whenever I'm ready. How will I know when I'm ready?" She sighed, then took a deep breath. "I have to start thinking about the baby. I have to figure out my options."

Soon after Troy had been deployed, Lily had happily e-mailed him that she was pregnant. *Maybe now her baby could help her through her loss,* Raina thought.

"Options for what?" Gina asked.

"I don't think I can stay in this apartment. It's so painful being here. We were going to buy a house as soon as Troy came home."

Raina and Angie's gazes connected at the same time. Angie gave a small nod.

"You shouldn't make impulsive decisions right now," Raina advised her. "You should weigh the pros and cons of each one. But if you decide you do want to move, you're welcome to move into the Victorian with me and Angie."

"You're serious?" Lily asked, surprised.

Both women said at the same time, "Yes, we are."

"There's only one problem. If I move in with you, then I'll have to move again when I have the baby in late March."

"Why?" Raina asked. "Won't you need babysitters?"

Lily looked from Angie to Raina, then over at Gina. "Are they kidding?"

"I don't think they are," Gina assured her with a smile.

"I'm a pediatric nurse," Angie reminded her. "I like babies. Just think of all the expert advice I can give you."

Lily actually gave her a small smile.

"We would love to have you, Lily," Raina reiterated. "And I'm a sucker for babies, too. Yesterday, Shep McGraw's baby stole my heart. When Manuel put his little arms around my neck—"

She stopped. No one had heard about her visit to Shep's. She'd kept it to herself.

Lily murmured, "Troy knew Shep. He bought supplies from him."

Raina had forgotten that, as a general contractor, Troy might have dealt with Shep.

"You were at Shep McGraw's?" Gina asked. "How did *that* happen?"

Lily piggybacked on that. "What did you do while you were there?"

Angie asked, "Didn't you do a procedure on his son Manuel recently?"

Raina held up her hand. "Whoa, now, everybody. I shouldn't have brought it up."

"But you did," Gina reminded her, "which probably means you want to talk about it."

"No, I don't. I just mentioned it because—"

"Because Manuel stole your heart," Angie filled in.

"I never should have brought it up," Raina murmured again.

Lily shook her head. "Don't be silly. I'm all for anything that helps me think about something else for a while."

Raina could see that, even though Lily was talking a good game, she wasn't going to be able to think of anything else but Troy for a very long time. Still, if this conversation would help distract her a little… "I think Shep was nervous about Manuel's procedure and his care afterward. When he found out I was finished for the day, he invited me to go along and see his ranch. I did, and somehow his two boys, Joey and Roy, asked me to come back on the weekend. We went on a trail ride. It was really a nice afternoon."

"Nice?" Gina asked with a raised brow. "Does that mean you like Shep McGraw?"

"Shep's an old-fashioned cowboy." She felt herself blushing. "We're very different."

"Are you going to see him again?" Lily asked.

"I don't know. I don't know if I'm ready. And he has his hands very full with those three boys. I don't think a lasting involvement is on his mind right now."

"He's the love 'em and leave 'em type?" Angie asked.

"I've heard rumors. But for the past year, all I've seen is that he's trying to be a good dad."

"Taking in three boys from foster care is noble," Gina agreed.

Raina noticed that Lily was staring out the picture window, no longer hearing the conversation that swirled around her.

Raina touched her friend's hand. "Would you rather we left you alone? Or should we try to come up with a meal we can all make and enjoy together tonight?" She knew Lily might have a tendency to forget to eat and that wouldn't be good for her, especially because of the baby.

Lily saw through that ploy right away. "You're trying to take care of me."

"No," Gina protested, "we're trying to help you take care of yourself."

Lily looked from one of them to the other and then her gaze fell on a picture of Troy in his uniform that was sitting on a side table. "All right," she decided, pushing herself up from the couch. "Let's comb my cupboards for something exotic we can make."

Raina knew exotic wouldn't help Lily stop missing her

husband—it wouldn't help her forget she was a widow. But cooking a meal with her friends could be a start.

As Shep sat in an examination room at the Family Tree Health Center the following Wednesday, one thought kept racing through his mind—he should have kissed Raina when he had the chance.

He felt awkward now, sitting here while she examined Manuel. And he hadn't felt awkward at any time on Saturday. Not even after he'd almost kissed her.

Shep waited until she stopped examining Manuel's right ear. "We had a good time on Saturday." When she met his gaze without hesitation, he added, "*I* had a good time on Saturday."

"I did, too," she admitted.

Shep's blood ran faster. The exam room suddenly got hotter.

Breaking eye contact, Raina crouched down to Manuel. "You were such a good boy for me today. How about a sticker for your shirt?" She reached over to the counter, grabbed a strip of stickers and held it out to Manuel. "Can you point to the one you'd like?"

Manuel glanced up at her and then back at the stickers. He pointed to one of a cowboy and a horse, with a rope that sparkled with glitter.

"Good choice," she assured him with a smile, peeled it off its backing and put it on the right side of his shirt.

He kicked his legs and said "Horsey," then ran his finger over the silver rope.

"So he's healing like he should?" Shep asked.

"He's doing great. If there aren't any problems, I won't need to see him for three months."

Three months might be okay for Manuel, but it wasn't for Shep. He cleared his throat. "So you enjoyed the trail ride?"

Her arm around Manuel, she met Shep's gaze again. "Yes."

"How about you and I go on a trail ride together *without* pint-size chaperones?"

She looked surprised. Before she could say no, he added, "Maybe we could pack a picnic and explore Red Creek a little more. What about your day off?" He was keeping it light, easy and as casual as he could.

Raina hesitated. "I have two surgeries tomorrow morning, but then I don't have office hours for the rest of the day."

"Tomorrow?" It took him a moment to wrap his head around that. He thought he'd have time to get prepared, to ready himself for the idea. But then again, he didn't want her to change her mind.

He'd been leaning against the wall, arms crossed over his chest. Now he unfolded them and approached the table where Manuel was seated. Raina was wearing a smock printed with cartoon characters today. Underneath, a pale pink silky blouse was tucked into cream slacks.

This close to her, the rush of heat targeted very strategic parts of his body. "Can I ask you something personal?"

"You can ask."

"Have you dated since your husband passed on?"

"No, I haven't. Some of my friends in New York thought I should, but I couldn't. I guess I just wasn't ready."

"And now?"

"Are we going on a date?" she asked with a half smile that revved up his libido even more.

He chuckled. "That's a fair question. I'd like to think of it as one, if that doesn't rattle you too much."

"If I just think of it as a picnic and trail ride, I won't get rattled."

"Are you sure?" He gazed deeply into her eyes and could feel the undeniable attraction pulling between them.

She ducked her head.

But he wouldn't let her get away with that. He gently put his thumb under her chin, and she raised her gaze to his once more. "I think we should call a spade a spade," he said.

"Or a date a date?" she teased.

"Yeah."

After a hesitant moment, she asked, "What time do you want me there?"

"Whenever you're done here." He dropped his hand to his side, wanting to smooth his fingers over her cheek...brush her hair behind her ear...taste her lips.

She was looking at him as if she might want to do the same. "I'll make sure my cell phone is charged this time." Then she confided, "Shep, the boys made it easy last Saturday. When it's just you and me... I haven't dated for a *very* long time."

"I hear it comes back easily. It's just like riding a horse. You never forget how." Then he did touch her again. He just couldn't help it. He brushed the back of his hand over her cheek. "We're just going to spend a little time together, Raina. We can talk, ride, hike— whatever we want. No pressure. No expectations."

"That sounds good."

"Wide horsey?" Manuel asked, interrupting them.

Shep lifted his son from the table, held him up in the air and made him squeal. "You're a little young for a horsey. At least a real one. Maybe at Christmas, Santa will bring you a make-believe one."

Gathering Manuel into his arms, Shep carried him to the door. He was already looking forward to tomorrow.

No pressure. No expectations. For either of them.

Raina had been jittery on the drive to Shep's. But now, as they stood in the corral, the jitters were gone because she was worried he'd change his mind. He'd seemed distracted ever since she arrived. She wasn't going to stay if he didn't want to go on this trail ride.

He held the reins to her horse for her so she could mount. But she didn't. Instead, she said, "I know you probably have a hundred other things you need to be doing."

He looked surprised at her comment. "Why do you say that?"

"Because you seem far away. I don't want to keep you from—"

"You're not keeping me from anything." He rubbed his hand over his face and gazed at her with consternation. "You're too—"

"Perceptive?" she filled in sweetly.

He laughed then, a genuine laugh. "That's one of the words for it."

She waited, already knowing Shep used an easy grin and warm humor to deflect a discussion he didn't want to have.

"I'm concerned about Joey," he admitted. "But being

concerned about him isn't going to change anything right now, so let's just head into the sun and enjoy being alive." As soon as the words came out of his mouth he grimaced. "I always step into it with you, don't I?"

"Shep, you don't have to watch what you say. I'd like nothing better right now than to ride with the sun on my face."

He stepped toward her slowly, as if he wanted to touch her. In fact, she thought he might play with the tips of her hair as he had once before. Excitement—and apprehension—tingled through her down to her fingertips, and she knew that was because she'd like to touch him, too.

But instead of reaching toward her, he took a step back. "Do you need a leg up?"

"No. As long as you hold Lazybones, I'll be fine." Though she didn't know if she really would be. Her hands were shaking now. She couldn't recall the last time a man had made her feel exactly like this.

She reached for the saddle horn, put her foot in the stirrup and took a hop up all at the same time. She was in the saddle now, but Shep was standing beside her, just in case she'd have a problem climbing up. She considered herself a supremely independent woman. Yet Shep's protective manner made her feel feminine and looked after.

Their horses walked side by side as they rode out of the corral. A whispery breeze lifted her hair, brushed her face and seemed to cleanse her. The week of surgeries, appointments, her concern about Lily—it all seemed to shed from her shoulders until she felt renewed.

Shep kept pace with her as they soaked in the brush and the crooked fence line, the end-of-summer colors. One field was still dotted with yellow flowers. In the distance she caught sight of the fields of white cotton, and farther away, wind turbines that seemed to stand like protective sentinels. All of it was Texas now, the old and the new, the wild and the tame.

As she turned toward Shep at the same time he glanced at her, she realized he was still part of the wild side of Texas, even though on the outside he sometimes seemed tame. Was that why he excited her? Was that why she could forget the past when she looked into his blue eyes and got lost in a sensual haze? Tall, with a physique that showed he wasn't afraid of hard work, he rode a horse as if he were one with it.

They rode along the same trail they'd taken with the boys, but when they reached the creek they turned east instead of west.

"I know a spot," Shep said, "where the horses will be happy. There's a clearing for a picnic and more wild-flowers than brush. I stuffed one of those NASA space blankets into the saddlebag, too, so we won't have to worry about ants crawling on our plates."

She laughed. "You thought of everything. Do you do this often?"

"I bring the boys out here a lot. They think walking along the creek is pure fun. But it's a chance for me to teach them about marking a trail, learning what plants to stay away from—things like that."

Shep seemed to know that the best ways to parent were the most subtle. But she often got the impression he wasn't sure at all about how he was handling his sons. Was it because he hadn't had a good role model?

That was none of her business, especially since he'd shied away from talking about his childhood.

Shep led them through tall grass, sage and tiny yellow flowers, where butterflies darted here and there. Riding beside Shep, Raina couldn't imagine a more beautiful day.

Eventually he slowed and pointed ahead. "We can climb down here and tether the horses under those trees."

Shep quickly dismounted and stood by Raina's side, making sure she hopped to the ground safely. Standing close by, he waited until she was safely on the ground, then tethered the horses. The clearing under pecans and cottonwoods seemed to be a peaceful bit of paradise, as the creek water rushing over rocks into a natural dam sent crystal spray into the breeze.

"Would you like to hike first, or eat first and then work it off?"

"Maybe we could just sit and talk for a while and then decide."

Shep gave her a long look. "Anything in particular you want to talk about?" He sounded a bit wary.

"Not really. I thought maybe you could tell me what the problem was with Joey."

"You really want to hear that?"

"They're good kids, Shep. If there's anything I can do to help, I'd like to."

After he gave her another studying look, he nodded. "Let me get that blanket so the grass doesn't poke us."

She had to smile. Shep was definitely a practical man, and she appreciated that.

Once he'd spread the silver blanket on the ground, they settled under a canopy of leaves. Raina kicked off her boots and tucked her legs beneath her. "So tell me what's wrong. You really seemed worried this morning."

Shep stared into the creek, then brought his gaze to hers. "Last week the nurse from the school called me. She said Joey didn't feel well. He had a stomachache. So I picked him up and brought him home. He was mopey for a couple of hours but then seemed to be fine. I thought maybe he'd eaten something he shouldn't have."

"No fever or other symptoms?"

Shep shook his head. "No. I took his temperature. I watched him that day and the next. But he ate okay. He played with his brothers and didn't act sick."

"Did something else happen?" she asked.

"Yeah. Monday he didn't want to go to school. He said his stomach hurt again. He cried and threw a fit, so I let him stay home. But something about it just didn't feel right, so I took him in to see Tessa Rossi."

"Tessa's got a good eye, and she's thorough."

"Yeah, she is. She examined him and asked him a list of questions. She didn't find anything. She said we could run a bunch of tests, but I hate to put him through that without good cause. Especially when she thinks something else could be going on."

"Like something at school?" Raina guessed.

"Possibly. I don't know. I can't get him to talk to me. And Roy is just as close-mouthed. If he knows anything, he's not saying."

"Did you speak with Joey's teacher?"

"That's next on the list. I have a phone conference with her tonight."

Raina couldn't help moving a little closer to Shep, reaching out and touching his arm to offer comfort. But as soon as she did, everything changed between them. Instead of just engaging in friendly conversation, she felt connected to him in an elemental way. Her heart beat so fast she could hardly breathe, and the air around them seemed electrified.

Somehow, she managed to find a few words. "You'll figure it out."

The blue of his eyes had suddenly deepened. She knew he, too, felt the change in the air between them.

His voice was husky when he said, "This could be up to Joey. If he can't trust me, it's going to be hard going for us both."

Shep shifted, leaned forward and sandwiched her hand between his and his arm—his very strong forearm. "I didn't bring you out here today to talk about the boys."

After only a moment's hesitation, she asked, "Why *did* you ask me out here today?"

"Because I like you," he said simply. "And because when I'm with you, all I can think about is kissing you."

Her stomach did a flip. Her heart fluttered. The sun seemed even brighter and the sky even bluer.

"Say something," he muttered. "If you want me to get back on my horse and forget this conversation ever happened—"

"I don't want you to get back on your horse," she almost whispered.

He took off his hat and set it on the blanket, out of the way. When he leaned in closer to her, she closed her eyes.

But his mouth didn't cover hers. Instead, she felt his lips touch, whisper soft, slightly above her ear. "A kiss shouldn't be too quick." His voice was husky with desire.

"No?" she asked, her pulse pounding in her temples, her cheeks getting warm.

When he brushed his jaw against her cheek, she noticed only the slightest bit of stubble. The sensation was so erotic she felt her nipples harden.

His hand, still covering hers, now moved up her arm and under her hair. "If a man goes for a woman's lips right away, the kiss is over too fast. So I like to ease into it."

His lips brushed the corner of her mouth and her breaths came fast.

"Or would you rather just get it over with?" he asked against her mouth.

She shook her head, and when she did, her lips rubbed back and forth across his. Like flint on tinder, heat sparked. Suddenly they were kissing, with no chance to go back to slow and easy. He held her head with both hands as his tongue slid into her mouth.

Her response was instinctive and inflammatory. It had been too long since she'd felt like this. So long. Shep made her feel beautiful and desirable, protected and wanted. She let those feelings rule her as she wound her arms around his neck.

She couldn't seem to get enough of him. The kiss that had started easy, that had grown sensual, had now turned into raw hunger. The excitement of the moment and the heat they were generating drove them on.

Shep stretched out his long legs against hers. Side by side they held on to each other. She was driven by something she didn't understand, something she didn't want to think about right now. She just wanted to feel—feel like a woman, feel Shep, feel him touching her. He *would* touch her if she touched him.

She slid one hand under his shirt placket and unfastened the snap. Her fingertips met hair and bare skin.

Shep groaned and lifted her T-shirt to unfasten her bra.

Raina had never been impulsive, never been imprudent, not in her whole life. But now she felt reckless and invigorated and awake to her sensuality in a way she hadn't been for almost a decade. She wanted Shep's hands on her body. She wanted to know she was capable of responding. She needed this tough, enigmatic cowboy to make her come alive.

He seemed to need her, too. He invited her taunting caresses by murmuring, "That's it, Raina. That's exactly right."

When he'd given her breasts enough attention to make her grip his shoulders tightly, she cried, "I want more."

"More of this or more of something else?"

"More of *you*," she said almost mindlessly.

He unzipped her jeans and pulled them down far enough that he could insert his hand into her panties. Then he stroked her until she didn't have a coherent thought.

In a frenzy of desire now, they feverishly undressed each other. When they were both naked, Shep covered her body with his, kissed her once more and asked, "Are you ready?"

Her desire for Shep seemed to consume her. "Yes," she told him, breathlessly.

At first, Shep slowly guided himself inside her. She moaned, tasting passion, so hungry for it she could only arch up to him and clutch his shoulders, pleading for more. He plunged into her, and the speed at which they took each other robbed them both of all their breath. Raina's body wound tight, tensed and released with shattering tremors that made every nerve ending quiver. She felt Shep's climax end in a groaning shudder.

Raina held on to him tight, needing to feel his body against hers to prove what they'd just experienced had been real.

She was fine, really okay, until Shep rolled off her and onto his side. Then she closed her eyes and took a deep breath. Suddenly she had to blink fast to force away tears. But blinking didn't help.

So many emotions assaulted her—regret, confusion, guilt, pent-up feelings of loss. Yet joy and tingling pleasure were still alive in her body from Shep's touches, caresses and kisses.

What had she done?

Giving in to feelings she couldn't push back, she finally had to let her tears run down her cheeks, because they had nowhere else to go.

Chapter Five

"What's wrong?" Shep asked, looking horrified that he'd caused this reaction in her.

Raina couldn't stop her tears long enough to tell him none of this was his fault. She couldn't even catch her breath.

Really worried when she didn't answer, he rolled to his side. "Did I hurt you?"

"No!" The word was a burst of emotion into the stillness of the peaceful day.

"Then what's wrong?"

She shook her head and just held up her hand to signal she needed a few moments to figure it all out.

Quickly, he pulled on his briefs and jeans and buckled his belt. Then he waited without touching her.

She figured she'd spooked him as much as she'd spooked herself.

He handed her her panties and jeans and didn't look away as she dressed, obviously determined to find out what was going on. Eventually, after she'd adjusted her bra and rebuttoned her blouse, her tears slowed.

Thoughts zipped through her mind and she said the first one that found its way to her mouth. "This was a mistake. I shouldn't be here with you."

The lines along Shep's mouth became more pronounced, and she could tell he was restraining his response. "Why?" he asked, calmly.

She was grateful for his calm. If he had turned angry or frustrated or impatient, she probably would have kept all her thoughts to herself. But Shep's concerned blue eyes and his gentle waiting urged it to all pour out.

"Do you know what the date is?" Without waiting for him to answer, she continued, "It's September ninth, and Saturday is September eleventh."

"Raina."

The caring in his voice undid her even more. "You don't understand," she said, before he could say he did. "I know it's been nine years, and I didn't think another anniversary would be so raw. But it's not just Clark and what happened to him and all the others. It's the memories of everything about it—going to the Family Assistance Center, applying for the death certificate, forever hearing the fire bell clang at the Ground Zero memorial service. And most of all, the finality of that sound." She shook her head, as if that could stop the memory. "Every year I remember the private memorial service we had, too. Clark's friends and relatives told stories and I made a collage of pictures. His brother pieced together videos of him."

She took a deep breath and pushed her hair back from her face with both hands.

"Tell me about it," he requested, as if he sensed more was bubbling up inside her and could form a thick wall between them if she didn't let it out.

After a long silence, sorting out the words that could express all of it, she said in a low voice, "I didn't go to class. I hardly ate. My mom stayed with me for a while, but I sent her home. Everyone kept saying they were sorry, and I didn't know what to say back. I just couldn't make sense of it."

She turned to face Shep. "When I finally returned to class, I was like a robot. But then the pace and complexity of med school gave me a routine to hold on to. Weeks and months passed, and I had a goal—to become the doctor Clark wanted me to be. That was all I thought about and all I lived for. It was my way of holding on to his memory. As the years passed, I found a rhythm. I concentrated on children and I helped them. By helping them I helped myself."

The burble of the creek and a call of a bird were the only sounds until Shep asked, "Why did you come back to Sagebrush?"

"Because I knew that to move on, I couldn't stay in New York. So I came back home to be near my family, to share a practice and make a difference here." She had told a bit of this to her friends, but had never let it pour out to this extent. Why had the dam fully burst open with Shep?

His hand clasped her shoulder for a few moments, and then, as if the contact was still too incendiary, he took his hand away. "I never meant for things to get so out of hand today."

She could hear the sincerity in his voice, still feel the warmth of his hand where it had lain. "I know you didn't. I never expected—" She dropped her face into her hands for a moment, then glanced at him again. "This isn't *me,* Shep. As I told you, I haven't dated since Clark died. I've just ignored that side of me. Yet, when I came out here today, I felt so alive, and the place is so beautiful, and you— I hadn't felt a connection like that in a very long time. I wasn't thinking of the anniversary date. I guess, subconsciously, I just wanted to feel alive." She let out a long sigh. "And that's why it happened."

"And afterward, why the tears?" he probed. "Because I wasn't your husband?"

Closing her eyes, she thought about her reaction. "It's not that simple. I just got bombarded by all the emotions a woman feels when she joins with a man. Sex was never just a physical release for me, and I guess I'm too old for it to be now. I know it is for guys, but I'm just not wired like that. It seems odd that pleasure and joy should let everything else crash in, but that's what happened."

"I knew you weren't the kind of woman to have recreational sex," he admitted. "That's why I've kept my distance. I've got three boys who need me. I'm not looking to partner up and make my life more complicated than it is."

Partner up. Was she relieved he didn't want to? Or hurt he didn't want to? What she was, was confused. "That's honest," she murmured, glad he could be.

"You were honest with me. I thought I should return the favor."

He'd already told her he didn't trust women. She'd sensed from the beginning that he was a loner and intended to run his life without having to answer to anyone else. They'd made a huge mistake today, and they both knew it.

"Do you want to go back?" he asked her.

She knew if she said "Let's have a picnic" they would have it, no matter how awkward it would be. But why put them through it? Why put them through having to make small talk and pretend they hadn't been as intimate as two people could be?

"That would probably be best," she responded, and saw the relief in his eyes. Whatever had been brewing between them had ended today—because neither of them were ready for it.

On Saturday, Shep leaned against the kitchen counter, trying to look more relaxed than he felt as Manuel's caseworker inspected his cupboards and refrigerator.

He hated these visits, but he knew they were necessary. Still, he felt one wrong move, one wrong word and she could swoop Manuel out of their lives.

"Did you find what you're looking for?" he asked, with some attempt at levity.

Uncharacteristically quiet, Roy and Joey sat at the kitchen table eating lunch. Manuel poked at the noodles on his tray, smearing cheese on the vinyl and then across his mouth.

Carla Sumpter, a tall brunette in her forties, gave a weary sigh. "Mr. McGraw, you know this is just routine. Could I have a word with you on the porch while the boys finish their lunch?"

Manuel suddenly decided he'd had enough of lunch. "Daddy, Daddy. Up! Up!"

Ignoring Carla for the moment, Shep went to Manuel, lifted him from his high chair and took him to the sink, where he proceeded to wash his hands and face. Manuel shook his head from side to side, avoiding the damp paper towel, but Shep made a game of it and soon the little boy was giggling.

"Mr. McGraw." The caseworker reminded him she was there.

He faced her and said, "The boys come first, even before your report. Just give me a few seconds and I'll come out on the porch with you." Crossing to the table, he said to Roy and Joey, "Each of you can have two cookies from the bakery box. I know how many are in there, so don't try to fool me." He winked at them. "I'll be right outside."

Roy crooked his finger at Shep.

Shep leaned down toward him.

Roy asked, "She's not going to take Manuel with her, is she?"

Roy asked this every time the caseworker visited. "No, she's not. Now eat a cookie and drink your milk. I'll be back."

Two minutes later, he was standing on the porch with Mrs. Sumpter. He took his key ring out of his pocket and handed it to Manuel to keep him occupied.

Shep had to admit he was distracted today. He had been for the past two days. In spite of his attempt, he hadn't been able to stop thinking about Raina. Especially today—September eleventh. He'd thought about calling her. But his gut told him to leave her alone—for now. In a few weeks, he'd have to check on her. They hadn't used protection, and he would have to find out if she was or wasn't pregnant.

Although images of Raina and their day together had kept him awake the past two nights, he shifted his focus to Manuel.

Carla wiped a little smear of cheese from Manuel's cheek with her forefinger, and he grinned at her. She smiled back. "I'm glad his operation went well. He does seem to be hearing better. You said your housekeeper is shopping today?"

"Yes. Some sale she wanted to go to in Lubbock. She'll be driving to Amarillo later in the month to see her sister. She needs a few things for that."

"How long will she be away?"

"Three or four days."

"And you think you can handle all three yourself?"

"I spend as much time with them as Eva does." He tried to keep his voice from showing his impatience. "When she leaves after supper, it's me and them. On her days off, it's me and them. Believe me, Mrs. Sumpter, we'll be just fine when she's away."

She peered inside the kitchen where Roy and Joey were comparing the size of their cookies. Then her gaze returned to Manuel again. With her purse under her arm, she descended the steps. "I hope so, Mr. McGraw. I do hope so."

As he watched her make her way to her car, he looked forward to the day when her visits would end. He looked forward to the day when he was officially Manuel's dad.

Smoothing his hand over his little boy's hair, he thought of Raina again and how good she was with his boys. Did they need a mother?

Not as much as they needed one stable person in their lives who would never leave them. Shep knew he was that person.

For the past few days, Raina had told herself not to panic. Yes, her period was late. But it could just be…stress.

The problem was—she was never late. Never, ever. Not even through the most horrible time of her life.

So she'd done what any woman in this position would do. She'd gone out and bought two pregnancy tests last night on her way home. Angie had just switched to the day shift and left for work. Raina was alone in the house.

Despite reminding herself once again not to panic, she still was. A few minutes later, she waited in the bathroom, staring at the thermometerlike stick lying on the vanity. She read the code on the display window.

Her head swirled as she realized what the message meant. She was pregnant. Hurriedly, she unwrapped the second package, hoping the first was a mistake and would say something different.

But deep down she already knew the reading was true. She was carrying Shep's baby.

It would take a few minutes until her world righted itself and she could figure out what she was going to do next.

"You're pregnant?" Ryder Greystone's voice was filled with astonishment.

"That's what I said." Raina sat quietly beside her brother on his patio Sunday evening, looking up at the sky, trying to decide what to do.

"Who's the father?" Her brother's voice was gruff,

and she knew this was hard for him. He'd always been the kind of big brother who wanted to take care of his little sister.

"Shep McGraw." Raina explained how she'd met Shep and the boys.

"I heard he was adopting three boys. What's his story? Why did he do it?" As a cop, as a detective, Ryder was always looking for motives.

"He was born in this area. Then he and his mom moved to California after his dad died. He ended up in the foster-care system there. He insists his goal is to give kids more than a temporary home, a home like he never had."

"So this guy blows into town, buys a ranch, a lumberyard, and adopts a few kids. I think I'll do a background check."

"Ryder."

Ryder's suspicions stemmed from the fact that he'd seen his share of domestic violence, as well as women harmed by con men. But Shep didn't fit into either category.

"Just let me check around, Raina. I don't want you getting involved with someone you shouldn't get involved with. And don't lecture me on how you have to live your life on your own terms. Go ahead, do that. Just let me be in the background making sure those terms are good ones. You deserve the best. And if this guy isn't the best, you need to know."

"He's a wonderful dad. I think that tells a lot about a man."

"How long have you been dating him?"

That one was hard to answer. She didn't want her brother to know their first date had ended in making love under a cottonwood. "Ryder, Shep and I connected. It happened fast."

"You're not impulsive."

"I was this time. Isn't that obvious? We didn't use protection. We didn't even think about protection."

"Too much information," Ryder said with a shake of his head.

"You were grilling me. I get confused between an interrogation and what a brother should know."

He chuckled. "Raina, sometimes I don't know what to do with you."

"Just don't tell Mom yet. Once I know what I'm going to do—" The cell phone in her purse beside her chair beeped. She plucked it out, thinking it might be Lily. However, the number on the screen was Shep's. Her heart started beating even faster than it had when she'd told Ryder her news as she answered the call.

"Hi, Shep." That was lame, but she didn't know what else to say, not yet anyway.

"Raina, hi. How are you?"

"I'm fine." Had he called for that reason? Had he called to see if she was pregnant?

"I don't know if I believe you. You weathered September eleventh okay?"

Had he been thinking about her that Saturday? It sounded as if he had been. "I weathered it." She didn't want to go into it now, with her brother listening.

"I thought about calling you. But it seemed better just to let everything…settle."

She knew exactly what he meant. "Is that why you called tonight?"

"I called for more than one reason. But I don't want

to talk about them on the phone. For starters, do you by any chance have the name of a nurse I could call who would come to stay with the boys overnight?"

That question hadn't even been on her clipboard. "A nurse? Why do you need a nurse?"

"I don't need a nurse per se, but I've got a sick horse, and Eva's away in Amarillo. I might be able to take Roy and Joey to the barn with me and let them sleep in bedrolls, but I can't do that with Manuel. All I would need is the caseworker showing up and finding out about it. So I've got to do this right."

"You have to stay with the horse all night?"

"Possibly. He has colic. I don't want to lose him."

An idea rolled around in her head, and she knew she should dismiss it. But she did need to talk to Shep, and at least she'd have a reason for being at the ranch. Before she changed her mind, she said, "I'm not on call this weekend. Why don't I come out and stay overnight with the boys and get them ready for school in the morning. Do you think that would be okay with them?"

"I'm sure that would be fine with them, but are you sure you want to do it?"

She knew what he meant. When she'd left his ranch, she'd had no intention of seeing him again. Or he her. But now everything had changed. "We do need to talk. Besides, I've missed the boys."

"They asked me about you, when you'd be coming to the ranch again."

"What did you tell them?"

"The truth. That I didn't know."

She could just blurt out the fact that she was pregnant. But that wasn't the way to handle this. She didn't know exactly what was—she just knew that wasn't the way. "I'm at Ryder's now. I'll have to go back home to pick up a couple of things. But then I'll be there. It will probably take about a half hour."

"You're a godsend, Raina. Thanks for offering to do this. If you have second thoughts on your way, though, and you can think of the name of someone else to call, let me know."

"I'll be there, Shep."

"A promise?"

"A promise." She could almost see his crooked smile as she closed the phone.

"You're driving out there tonight?" Ryder asked with a bit of disapproval in his tone.

"Shep has a sick horse and needs help with the boys. He can't leave them alone."

"I thought he had a nanny."

"She's away."

"How much older is she than he is?"

"Ryder!"

"How much?" he grumbled.

"About fifteen years. There's nothing going on between them except respect and affection."

"I'm still going to do a background check."

"I don't want you to. You're not going to find anything. He's a good man."

"Men who have been away for years and then return have a past. In that past, sometimes there are secrets."

Did Shep have secrets? Didn't everybody?

Standing, she went over to her brother and hugged him. "Please, Ryder. Just let me live my life. Okay?"

He didn't answer her.

Straightening, she picked up her purse and shoved the strap over her shoulder. "Remember, don't tell Mom anything."

"You *are* going to tell her you're pregnant."

She sighed. "In good time. I have to figure out what I'm going to do first."

"Keep in mind one thing, will you?" he asked soberly.

"What's that?" She thought he might insist she didn't have to be involved with Shep McGraw simply because she was carrying his child.

He told her something else. "I want you to think of yourself this time, Raina."

She wasn't sure what he meant. "Do you want to explain that?"

"When you married Clark, you supported his lifestyle as a fireman. You fit yours around it. After Clark died, you thought about his family, about his friends, about grants you could give to fire companies in his name, instead of using that money to make your life easier and secure."

"I used some to finish med school. That was all I needed."

"I know what you used. You needed a lot more than you gave away. The fact is, I don't think you really thought about yourself until you moved back here. Don't stop now. You consider what's best for you and your baby."

"I will," she promised him, already focused on the life growing inside of her. She would always do what was best for her baby.

Parking next to the veterinarian's van, Raina closed her car door. As she began walking toward the house, Shep strode across the lane from the barn, holding Manuel.

Roy and Joey were tight on his heels. Roy asked in excitement, "Are you going to put us to bed tonight?"

"I think I am."

Her gaze met Shep's and the world shook a little, a leftover seismic tremor from what had happened between them that day under the cottonwoods.

"Thanks for coming."

She felt herself blushing, something she couldn't remember happening before she'd met him. "Have you been trying to take care of the kids, the ranch and a sick horse all by yourself?"

"I'm definitely not super-rancher," he said with a crooked grin. "The man who tends to the horses most days stayed late. He just left when the vet arrived. I do know my limits."

In a way, she guessed that Shep thought he didn't have many limits. She wasn't sure what had given her that idea. He seemed to be able to tackle anything, and do a good job of it, whether it was adopting the boys or seeing to the ranch and handling the lumberyard business. She considered what Ryder had said about doing a background check and she liked the idea even less now than she had earlier. She'd have to tell him again to let it go.

As they started toward the house, Roy tucked his little hand in hers and a warm feeling enveloped her. She hadn't thought much about being a mother over the past few years—not since losing Clark. Now, with Roy's hand in hers, and the knowledge that she had a little life growing inside of her, she realized a forgotten dream could come true.

Once they were on the porch, she held out her hands to Manuel. He pursed his lips, made a sound like an engine and then lunged toward her. She caught him with a laugh, holding him close.

When Shep touched her elbow, she felt a shaft of heat rush through her. "I might have to spend most of the night in the barn. In the morning, we can talk."

Raina nodded, her throat suddenly tight. All she wanted to do was blurt out the words and see Shep's reaction. Yet, on the other hand, she wanted to keep the secret to herself, just in case telling Shep would change her life in a way she didn't want. She wasn't sure what to expect from him. Just how well *did* she know him?

Ryder's point exactly.

"We can talk when the crisis is over."

"Sometimes there seems to be one after another."

Releasing her arm, he ran his hand over Manuel's hair. She wondered what kind of dad Shep would be with a daughter. Protective, that was for sure. Probably doting, too. But he already had three children. Would he want another? And if he did, then what? How would she handle having him in her child's life? In *her* life? Attraction was one thing. Parenting was another.

"The boys had showers before supper. You can skip Manuel's bath tonight, if you'd like."

"I don't mind. We'll make a playtime of it."

"I've been putting cotton in his ears in case he splashes. I have those little earplugs, too. They're on top of the chest in his room."

"I won't forget," she said, amused that he'd think she would.

"No, I guess not," he responded with some chagrin. "I'm just trying to think of anything that could crop up."

She raised her eyebrows. "I'm thirty-seven, Shep, and my coping skills are pretty good. Even if your boys throw me a curve, I'll try not to strike out."

He laughed at her sports imagery. "Okay, I get the picture." His gaze lingered on hers for a few more seconds, and that made her tummy shimmy—and not from evening sickness.

"I can show you to the guest bedroom upstairs—"

"We'll show her," Roy piped up. "It's next to ours," he explained to Raina.

Shep gave Roy a pat on the back. "Thanks. I know you and Joey will make Dr. Gibson feel right at home."

Showing Raina just how prepared he was, Shep pulled a card from his pocket. "That has my cell phone number on it. I'll have it with me. If you need anything, just call."

Again she nodded.

After a last, long look at her and Manuel, he said, "I'll see you in the morning, boys," turned and jogged down the steps, not stopping his fast pace until he reached the barn. There he tossed another look over his shoulder at her and disappeared inside.

During the rest of the evening, Raina played mom. She had to admit, giving Manuel a bath while Joey and Roy brushed their teeth and put on their pj's felt natural. After settling Manuel in his crib, she sat on the boys' twin bed, Joey and Roy on either side of her, and read them their favorite story. The words rolled off her tongue as if she'd read it before, but she hadn't. They laughed and asked her to read their favorite pages over.

As Joey leaned forward to point to a picture, a medal

on a chain swung from around his neck. Raina asked, "That's St. Christopher, isn't it?"

Joey's fingers closed around the medal. "Yeah, it is. My dad who died gave it to me. He said it would always keep me safe."

"I have one, too," Roy remarked, as if he didn't want to be left out. "Mine's in a box in my drawer. I was afraid I'd lose it. So my dad…" He hesitated. "My dad in the barn said that's best for now."

"I think your medals are wonderful remembrances," she said softly.

Obviously wanting to change the subject, Joey asked, "Can we get a drink of water?"

The brothers tried to stall their bedtimes, but finally they settled in, tired from a weekend full of activities with Shep. Joey had seemed quieter than Roy, but then he always was. She wondered about the stomachaches, if he was still having them, but didn't bring them up.

Before she'd given Manuel his bath, she'd deposited her backpack in the guest bedroom and hung her outfit for office hours the next day in the empty guest-room closet. Apparently Shep didn't have overnight visitors often.

After taking her own shower, slipping into feminine pink plaid boxers and a T-shirt, she lay on top of the covers with a magazine she'd brought along, thinking she'd read for a little while, just in case the boys didn't go right to sleep. However, she must have been as tired as they were, because she drifted off.

The next thing she knew, she felt a hand on her shoulder—a large, warm hand. Thinking she was dreaming, she leaned her cheek against the fingers, remembering Shep's sensual touches by the stream.

"Raina?"

His voice was husky, deep, louder than a dream.

Instantly, she came awake and found Shep leaning over her.

Chapter Six

The light from the hall cut a swath into the guest bedroom, putting Shep in silhouette as he gazed down at Raina.

The same look had been in his eyes before they'd made love. No, not made love. They didn't know each other well enough for that. Still, she couldn't have had sex with him if she hadn't felt a deep connection. Did he feel that connection, too? Or had it only been pleasure he'd been after—a relief from his life with his boys.

He dragged a wooden chair from alongside the bed and sat facing her. "It's around midnight. I wanted to make sure everything was okay up here."

"How's the horse?"

"Buttermilk is coming along. Ed came back to help out. He's walking him while I make us some coffee."

Shep was looking at her pink T-shirt, appraising her plaid boxer shorts. She'd left the window open and hadn't bothered to cover with the sheet. Now she felt a little uncomfortable, especially without a bra. "The boys are fine. I read them a story while Manuel fell asleep."

"How many glasses of water did they ask for?"

"Three, but they only got two."

He chuckled. "If I don't set a boundary, they'll test me until I draw one."

"Manuel's the sweetest baby, and since I was here last, he's picked up more words and syllables. The surgery worked—I don't think he'll be far behind at all."

Okay, they'd covered the subject of the boys, and now they both knew what was coming. The pulse in her ears was pounding hard.

She hiked herself up to a sitting position and laid the magazine to the side of the bed.

"How did you really cope with September eleventh?" Shep asked, real concern in his voice.

She shrugged. "I spent most of the day with my friend Lily. She lost her husband recently and she's pregnant. We definitely understand each other right now."

"Lily Wescott? I knew her husband. Troy was a great guy."

Raina thought about how life was one big circle… just like life in Sagebrush. "I called Clark's family. Angie and Gina came over, too, late that evening. We went through photo albums. I do that every year and allow myself to relive the pain and cry. I found if I don't, if I try to ignore the day, if I think everything's going to be okay, then it isn't. Grief has a way of bleeding upward from your heart through your whole body, so it's better just to take it on."

"You're a brave woman, Raina."

She shifted on the sheet, uncomfortable with his assessment. "No, I'm not brave. I've just learned what works for me. Lily will have to find her own way. In the meantime, we can support each other. That's what friends are for. She's thinking of moving into the Victorian, and that would be terrific. We'll all help her raise her baby." Raina suddenly felt the color drain from her face.

Apparently Shep noticed. "What is it?" He took her hand, and the gesture made her confession so much harder.

She slipped her hand from his, needing her wits about her. "I'm pregnant, Shep. Two pregnancy tests were positive."

He looked stunned for a moment, took off his Stetson, twirled it in his hands, then set it back on the top of his head. "I know this pregnancy is my responsibility as much as yours, but I need a little time to take this in."

That really wasn't the reaction she'd expected, but Shep often did the unexpected. "Okay. I'll go back to sleep up here, and you can think about it while you're walking Buttermilk."

He took her hand again and this time held on. "I don't want you to feel alone in this, but right now I can't stay. I have to get back to the barn."

"I understand." And she did. But they couldn't resolve anything if they didn't talk. Obviously, Shep wasn't a big talker until he knew what he wanted to say.

Pushing back the chair, he stood, leaned down and kissed her forehead. It was a tender, light kiss, almost like a whisper. She might have imagined it.

After he put the chair back where it belonged, he went to the doorway. "Light off or on?" he asked.

"Off is fine. I need to go to sleep so I have energy for the boys in the morning."

"Remember, call me if you need me."

She had her phone on the bedside table and his number beside it. But she wasn't going to call him—because she didn't think he *wanted* her to need him.

Raina took the tray of cinnamon toast from the oven and carried it over to the table, where the boys were already starting on their scrambled eggs.

"What's that?" Joey asked.

"Cinnamon toast. My mom used to make it for me and my brother when we were your age. It's hot. I'll put a piece on your plates. You have to let it cool a little."

They had kept her stepping this morning—getting Manuel up, dressing him and readying the other two boys for breakfast, too. It was a challenge she'd enjoyed. The same thing with cooking breakfast. She hardly ever did that for herself, just grabbed a container of yogurt and a piece of fruit and ran.

She knew Shep was occupied with the veterinarian. As she cut pieces of cinnamon toast for Manuel, she wondered how the horse was faring. She wondered even more what Shep was thinking about her pregnancy.

A sudden knock at the door interrupted the boys' chatter. "Wait a couple more minutes before you try that toast," she warned them, and went to answer it. As soon as she opened it, the woman on the other side stepped back, surprised.

"Hello! I'm Carla Sumpter, Shep's caseworker. And you're…"

"I'm Raina Gibson." She could see in the caseworker's eyes that she instantly made a connection with information in Shep's file.

She wasn't sure whether to let the woman in or not. Maybe she should call Shep. But she didn't have to. Over Mrs. Sumpter's shoulder, she spotted him jogging toward the porch.

"Mrs. Sumpter! This is a surprise this early on a Monday morning. How can I help you?"

"I just thought I'd stop by for that follow-up visit and see how everyone is."

"Excuse me," Raina said. "I don't want to leave Manuel for too long."

The caseworker wouldn't need to talk to her, so she hurried back to the kitchen, where she put bite-size pieces of toast on Manuel's tray. He already had some scrambled eggs in his hair, and she tried to brush them away.

Roy looked up at Raina. "*Her* again?"

Raina tried to suppress a smile. "You don't like when she visits?"

Roy shook his head vigorously. "She puts ants in my pants."

Joey explained, "That means she makes us all nervous, especially Dad."

Raina had never seen Shep nervous, but then the boys probably sensed more than they saw.

As if on cue, the caseworker and Shep came into the

kitchen. "What are we having this morning?" Mrs. Sumpter addressed the boys.

"Something new," Roy told her. "Cinnamon toast."

"I see. Does Dr. Gibson cook for you often?"

Raina's mouth opened but she wasn't exactly sure what to say. She didn't have to worry because Roy filled in for her. "This is the first time. She stayed last night."

Shep's gaze met Raina's. "I explained about the horse being sick and you sleeping in the guest room."

"She gave Manuel a bath," Joey said helpfully.

"Wasn't that nice," Mrs. Sumpter said, even though Raina wasn't sure she meant it.

"Take another bite of toast, then get your things together," Shep ordered Joey and Roy. "You don't want to be late for the bus."

The brothers hurriedly took two more bites of toast, drank some milk and ran to the playroom to get their backpacks. The silence in the kitchen was awkward until they returned.

"I'll take them down the lane to the bus stop," Shep told the women. "If it's on time, I should be back here in about ten minutes. Will you be all right?" he asked Raina, in spite of Mrs. Sumpter being there.

She squared her shoulders and encouraged Manuel to eat another bite of toast. "I'll be fine."

Shep nodded to both women and led the boys to the door. After they called noisy goodbyes, they followed their dad to the bus stop.

In spite of the caseworker's attention focused on her, Raina pulled up a chair beside Manuel and offered him a sippy cup with milk.

"So. Mr. McGraw says you're Manuel's doctor," the caseworker said, prompting her.

"Yes. I've also treated Joey."

"And the two of you struck up a friendship?"

"You could say that."

"Now you're here, so I assume the two of you have some connection."

Oh, they had a connection all right, but she wasn't about to tell this woman about it.

"Are you planning to stay here while Eva is away?"

This woman was fishing. True, it was her job, but Raina still didn't like it. "No, I'm not. Shep called me and asked if I knew of a nurse who could stay overnight, and on such short notice, I volunteered myself. I've become fond of the boys."

"And Shep?"

"We respect and admire each other."

"How quaint."

Now Raina's hackles were up. "Excuse me?"

"Well, *admire* and *respect* are old-fashioned terms in a world that doesn't understand them very well."

Holding her temper, Raina returned, "That doesn't mean they can't exist."

"How old are you, Dr. Gibson?"

Taking a breath, warning herself to be tactful, she answered, "Thirty-seven."

"I assume you're single?"

"Yes. I'm widowed."

"You're young to be a widow. I assume your husband was the same age?"

"He was a few years older."

Apparently Mrs. Sumpter wasn't going to stop poking until she got the information she wanted. So Raina might as well put her life on the table. "Clark was a fireman. He died on September eleventh. I really don't want to discuss that with Manuel in the room."

"But he doesn't understand—" Mrs. Sumpter began.

Enduring enough, Raina interrupted her. "My former housemate is a baby-development expert. She believes children pick up mood and tone, as well as a sense that surrounds words when they're spoken. I remember that when kids are around. Maybe in your profession, it would be good if you did, too."

"I've been managing my job for fifteen years just fine."

"I'm glad about that. That should make Shep feel so much easier about adopting Manuel. I hope there won't be any surprises."

"That depends. If Shep is involved with you, the adoption could be delayed."

Footsteps on the porch were definitely Shep's this time. After entering the kitchen, he picked Manuel up out of his high chair. "How was breakfast, buddy?"

Manuel nodded and touched Shep's face with sugar-sticky fingers.

"Oh, so I'm going to wear cinnamon as aftershave this morning," he teased. He found a Busy Box for Manuel to play with on the table as the child sat on his lap.

Shep asked Mrs. Sumpter, "Why did you really come by this morning?"

"I'd like to finish up my questions first."

He glanced at Raina. "Does Raina need to stay?"

"Dr. Gibson is part of these questions. I want to know what the two of you are to each other."

Raina's heart felt like a high-speed train on a newly polished track.

Shep hadn't taken off his hat, and the shadow hid part of his face. "What if I told you we're trying to figure that out."

"I won't ask the obvious question, since you said you were in the barn all night and she was in the guest bedroom. But if you get married, that could add months onto the course of the adoption until we make a portfolio on Dr. Gibson. The relationship has to be examined to make sure it's healthy for Manuel."

Shep unbuttoned the top button of his shirt and looked angry. "You don't think Raina would be good for the boys?"

"I didn't say that."

"That's what you indicated. Don't you think they might need a woman's influence, kindness and warmth?"

"Every child deserves that, Mr. McGraw. But I have to see with my own eyes to know it's true. You have bonds with these boys. I know that. If Dr. Gibson is going to be in their lives, I have to see how they relate to her, too." She looked from Shep to Raina, and although they were sitting at least a foot apart, Raina wondered if the caseworker could feel the sexual tension between them. She herself certainly could. Whenever Shep was in the same room, everything seemed to buzz.

Mrs. Sumpter cast a final glance at Manuel. "All right. I think that's all I can do here today. You don't need to see me out. I can find the door. It was nice to meet you, Dr. Gibson. Maybe we'll see each other again sometime soon."

After the caseworker was gone, Raina heaved a sigh of relief. "That sounded like a threat."

"No, she just keeps her word. I'm sorry you had to go through that."

"Is she like that every time she comes?"

"She has a reason for each of her visits. This—" He pointed to her and then himself. "This just cropped up today, so she pounced on it. You handled her well."

"I told her what she wanted to know." Raina was a bit disgusted with herself about that.

"I imagine you just gave her the essentials. That was good."

"And what are the essentials, Shep? That we're friends? Is that what we are?"

The tension between them had coiled inside of her so tight that her chest hurt. She needed to know what Shep was thinking, whether or not he was going to be involved in her life and her—their—baby's.

An expression passed over his face that was something akin to determination. She didn't understand it until he rose with Manuel and settled him into his play saucer. Once the toddler was occupied, Shep stood right in front of her, staring down at her, big and looming and male. An excited thrill shot through her and, in a flash, she remembered being naked with him, joining with him, feeling guilty and confused because the pleasure had been so wonderful and taken her totally off guard.

"Marry me," he demanded, the two words jumping into the air as if he'd been waiting all night to say them.

Since they rammed into her, stealing her breath, she simply repeated them. "*Marry* you?"

His hands settled gently on her shoulders as if to

prevent her from running away. "You're carrying my baby. I want to be a dad to this child just as much as to Manuel, Joey and Roy. I want to be there when this baby's born. I want to see his or her first smile, first step, first everything. Manuel has changed and grown before my eyes, and I don't want to miss a minute of this new baby's life."

Raina swallowed hard. "I know you like being a father, Shep, but what about *us?*" Her mind was spinning with all the ramifications of what he was suggesting.

Shep's jaw tightened, as if what he was going to say was hard for him. "I've never been married. So I can only imagine what your husband meant to you, and I'm not aiming to pretend that what you and I have is anything like that. But I do know there's something between us. When we're together, we want each other. That's what led us to where we are now. We can build on that."

Did they have something to build on? As she'd told the caseworker, she respected and admired him. If she was truly honest with herself, she also had to admit she was falling for him. But *marriage?* "I don't know, Shep. I'm a doctor. I never imagined I'd settle down on a ranch."

Still clasping her shoulders, working his thumbs up and down her neck, he asked gently, "Are you panicked by the idea of having a baby?"

"A little."

"You don't have to be. You don't have to give up your career. Eva will help us. Our baby will have three brothers."

"But getting married might affect your adoption."

"Actually, I think it will help. You'll have to have interviews with Mrs. Sumpter and eventually appear with me before the judge. But I don't see why there would be a problem. Two parents are better than one, if they both love kids."

"You know I love kids, Shep. Yet I never imagined I'd be the mom of four—practically overnight."

"It *is* a lot to think about," Shep agreed. "I've been mulling it over in my head all night. But if you want a family and kids as much as I do, I think it's the best thing to do for all of us. But whatever you decide, I want to be a father to our baby…whether we're married or not."

Parental rights. Custody issues. A child being shuttled back and forth between two parents. How confusing would that be?

Raina considered her past nine years—her loneliness, her loss, her own childhood growing up without her father. Then she considered a life with Shep and his boys here on the ranch. In vivid recall, her tryst with him under the cottonwoods played like a movie in her mind. She could see in Shep's eyes that he was remembering, too, and he leaned forward to kiss her. His lips had almost settled on hers when Manuel began banging on his play saucer, tired of the toys there, tired of not being the center of attention.

Shep straightened, touched her cheek tenderly, then scooped Manuel from his saucer. "Marriage *is* a lot to think about. Our life together could be a challenge in a lot of ways. There's something else you might want to think about. We should have a prenup to protect us both."

Watching Shep with Manuel, studying the play of his muscles under his shirt as he hefted the toddler higher in his arms, she suddenly realized what the most challenging aspect of their marriage could be. Shep had said several times he didn't trust easily. What kind of marriage could they have without trust?

"I need time to think about all this."

Manuel leaned toward her, reaching his arms out. She lifted him and felt the joy of holding a baby, realized that in June she'd be holding *her* baby.

When her gaze met Shep's, she saw desire there…and hope. Could they have a life together?

Was she crazy for even considering his marriage proposal?

On the patio at the back kitchen entrance to the Victorian the following evening, Raina stood with Lily, looking over the yard at the purple-and-gold sunset. "I'm glad your bedroom furniture fit."

With a loud bang, Angie backed out of the screen door from the kitchen, carrying a small side table. "I think this will look great out here."

Lily gave them both a forced smile. "I should probably sell everything I put in storage, but I can't just yet."

Raina tugged Lily down to the glider rocker that had already been positioned on the patio. "You have to give yourself time. Don't do anything that doesn't feel right."

"Moving in here feels right."

"Good," Angie said. "Feel free to add whatever personal things you want. The house reflects all of us, though it might just be the two of us, once Raina makes her decision about Shep's proposal."

Last evening Raina had told Angie and Lily about Shep's proposal. Now it was time to tell them her decision. She'd been mulling over everything since yesterday.

"Do you two think I'm crazy if I say yes?"

"Depends on your reasons," Lily insisted, her full attention on Raina.

"First and foremost, I've always wanted a big family, and at thirty-seven I might not get another chance. And second, Shep is a wonderful father—those boys love him. Doesn't my baby deserve that? Doesn't *our* baby deserve two parents and a family atmosphere?"

She raised a third finger. "And the last reason is that Shep is a good man. I've been alone for so long, and he's the kind of man who makes me feel protected. I think we could have a good marriage." She blushed a little, remembering the passionate intimacy she'd experienced with Shep.

"You're really attracted to him, aren't you?" Angie asked.

"I am. I can't figure it out. My heart races and my stomach gets butterflies whenever he's close."

Lily spoke. "You've given us good reasons why marriage might work, but what do you feel about him? Because in the end, that's what's important."

"To be honest, I'm confused. All these years, I felt as if I was still married to Clark. It's hard to turn off that life to start a new one. I don't want to ever forget what we had, who he was, how brave he was—though I know I can't hold on forever. With this baby coming, I have to look forward."

"We'll be pregnant together," Lily said with a real smile.

Raina laughed. "Yes, we will." Then she became serious again. "But I feel if I do this, I'm deserting you when you've just arrived."

"That's nonsense," Lily assured her. "Angie will be here, and you and I can still see each other. It's not as if you're going to fall off the face of the earth."

"No, but handling three kids, plus having a new husband and being pregnant, is going to make for long days and maybe even long nights."

The women laughed.

"Don't forget about the horses," Raina added, getting a quiver in her stomach just thinking about all of it.

"Do you really want to marry Shep?" Angie asked her.

Raina hesitated, not knowing if she was making the right decision. But she answered, "Yes, I do."

"Do you think you'll move your things to his place?" Lily asked.

"I'm not sure. He already has a house full of furniture. I could move my bedroom suite to my mom's garage."

"That's silly," Angie decided. "Just leave whatever you don't move here, then if…well…if things don't work out, you'll have a place to come home to."

The three women had been totally involved in their conversation, so involved that all three of them were startled when a deep male voice beside the patio said, "Howdy, ladies."

Raina swung around. "Shep!"

"I rang the front bell but no one came. Then I heard voices from back here. I didn't mean to interrupt."

As Lily went over to Shep to introduce herself, Raina wondered how much of the conversation he might have overheard. What must he be thinking?

Lily said, "I'm Lily Wescott. I work at Family Tree with Raina. I just moved in today."

Shep gave Lily's hand a firm shake. "It's nice to meet you. I knew your husband and I'm so sorry for your loss."

Lily seemed to swallow hard, but managed to say, "Thank you."

Angie crossed to Shep now and he shook her hand, too. She smiled. "I'm Angie Rigoletti, a pediatric nurse at the hospital. I work with Raina now and then, and I moved in here in August."

"I see." He studied each of the women as if he was wondering about their bonds and what made them want to live together.

Lily and Angie exchanged a look and Raina wasn't surprised when Lily asked, "Angie, do you want to help me empty some boxes?"

"Sure thing," Angie agreed. Then she added, "We have a lot to do upstairs, so don't worry about us interrupting you."

Lily and Angie were through the kitchen door before Raina could blink.

"I didn't mean to chase them away." Shep stepped up onto the patio. "If this is a bad time—"

"No, it's not a bad time. I was going to call you."

"The boys have been asking me about you."

"Is that why you stopped over?"

"No," he replied. "I came to get your answer. I need to know what direction we're headed and what steps to take next."

What steps to take next—as far as custody went? Custody worried her as much as everything else. If he was really determined to be a father, he'd want equal rights to his child. She couldn't bear the thought of a son or daughter of theirs shuttling back and forth between two households. Her decision really was the best one to make for their baby.

"I've made my decision. But are you sure you want to consider marrying a stranger?"

He closed the distance between them, smiled his crooked smile and assured her, "You're *not* a stranger. You're my baby's mother."

"Our baby," she remarked, quietly. "And if your proposal still holds, yes, I'll marry you."

She wasn't sure what she thought would happen when she said the words, but nothing did, and that surprised her a little. Attraction was still rippling between them. She felt goose bumps on her arms whenever he looked deeply into her eyes, as he did now. But he was examining her expression and she wondered what that meant. She soon found out.

"I overheard part of your conversation when I was walking along the side of the house."

"Shep—"

He held up his hand to stop her. "Look, I know this is an unusual situation. But if I commit to this marriage, I want you to know I intend to make it work. So I guess my question to you is, do you intend to do the same? Leaving your furniture here is one thing. Leaving part of your resolve here is another."

She should have realized strength of commitment would be important to Shep. They really didn't know each other, yet he seemed willing to take this step without completely trusting her. What would that mean for their marriage? Could they learn to trust as well as learn to love? After all, she knew now she was falling in love with Shep. Otherwise, she couldn't do this.

"When I marry you, Shep, I'll do everything I can do make it work. Lily and Angie are good friends and they just want to be here for me, no matter what decision I make."

The silence that fell between them was a bit awkward. "When should we tell the boys?" Raina asked. She wished Shep would touch her. She wished he'd reassure her that this ready-made family would fulfill both their dreams.

"How about tomorrow night. Why don't you come over for dinner? Then we'll tell them." He ran a hand through his hair. "I've got to be getting back so Eva can leave. By the way, she's willing to stay on and help with the baby. I didn't know what you might want to do about your practice after the baby's born."

"I don't know yet, but I have some time to think about it."

"Yes, you do. And we have a lot to talk about."

Did Shep mean practical things like prenuptial agreements, nannies and four children to raise? Or did he mean they had a lot to discover about each other?

She saw the heat in Shep's eyes before he reached for her. Then his arms were around her and his lips were on hers, firm and demanding, and a little more possessive than they'd been before.

All too soon, he pulled away and cleared his throat. Then he touched his lips to her forehead and murmured, "Good night, Raina."

The sensation of his lips on her skin was so sensual, she savored it for a moment. When she opened her eyes, she caught a glimpse of Shep's back as he headed around the side of the house.

What had she done?

Chapter Seven

"We're getting married," Shep told his sons the following evening, as Raina held her breath in anticipation of their reaction. She thought the boys liked her, but with children, you never knew what they were thinking.

Roy immediately clapped his hands, jumped up and down and ran to her. "Are you going to be our mom?"

"No," Joey answered before she could. "She's just marrying our dad. She'll be our *step*mom."

Raina didn't think now was the time to split hairs. She didn't know what would happen with Manuel's adoption, whether it would go forward with just Shep, or if she would be included. They'd be sitting down with the caseworker soon to discuss that.

So she simply said, "I'd like you to think of me as your mom."

"That's all right, isn't it?" Roy asked his older brother.

But Joey didn't look so sure. "I guess so."

Raina saw that Shep had been right in his decision not to tell them about the baby yet. This change was enough for now. She hugged Roy, crossed to Joey and knelt down before him. "It's a big decision, whether you want somebody for your mom or not. So you could just call me Raina until you decide."

"Instead of Dr. Gibson?" Joey looked to Shep for confirmation.

"If that's what Raina wants, then that's what you can do," Shep said, looking approving at how she was handling this. His approval meant a lot to her, and that surprised her.

"So you're going to live here with us?" Joey wanted to make sure he had it right.

"After we get married, I will. We're not sure when that will be yet, but we'll let you know. Tonight, I just came over to cook dinner with you. Your dad says you like tacos."

"I love tacos," Joey replied, still with a bit of wariness.

"I make my own salsa. Do you want to help?"

Again Joey looked at Shep, and Shep gave a nod. With a roll of his shoulders, he agreed. "Okay."

Apparently, Joey still firmly had his guard in place. She hoped this new situation wouldn't make his walls even sturdier. Only time would tell what was in store for all of them.

Manuel had toddled over to her and now wrapped his arms around her legs.

She stooped and picked him up. "Do you want to help, too?"

Roy made the decision for his little brother. "He can taste it."

They all laughed, and Raina hoped this was going to be the start of their new family life. It might be different from her first marriage, but just as fulfilling in its own way.

The preparations for supper were noisy and fun, with Shep exchanging glances with her often. Those glances held questions and doubts and anticipation and excitement.

After dessert, she and Shep played board games with the boys, and spin-the-top with Manuel. They put the toddler to bed first, then read stories to Roy and Joey. Finally, everyone was tucked in for the night.

They were almost out the door when Joey called Shep back in.

Raina gave them some privacy and went downstairs. She straightened up a bit, surprisingly feeling as much at home here as she did at the Victorian. Afterward, she stood at the coffee table and looked around the room, letting its warm, comfortable ambiance seep into her.

When Shep came downstairs, he found her like that and asked, "Looking for something?"

"Nope."

His face sobered. "I guess I should have asked what you want to change."

She crossed to him, feeling their attraction wrap around her as she gazed into his blue eyes. "I was looking at it through a mom's eyes, or trying to. I wouldn't change a thing."

His brows arched, and he seemed surprised at her answer. "Most women would want to come in here and redecorate."

"I'm not most women, Shep, and I don't think you'd be marrying me if I was. You've done a fine job with the place. Everything's comfortable and sturdy and made for boys. The decorations speak of your Texas heritage."

Taking her hand, he brought it to his lips and kissed each of her fingertips. She felt shivery all over. But they weren't married yet, and they still had a lot to talk about until they were.

"What did Joey want, or is that a private matter?"

"Nothing too private. He just asked me if you were going to sleep here overnight again."

"What did you tell him?"

"I told him, after we were married, you'd be moving in here and we'd be sleeping in the same bedroom. I thought I might as well be honest about it."

"Did he ask any more questions?"

"No, he just turned over and went to sleep."

After Shep led Raina to the sofa, he sat beside her. "We should go to the courthouse and fill out the applications for a license next week. How do you feel about that?"

"That would be fine."

"If you want a church wedding, we could wait."

"I don't need a church wedding, Shep." She saw a flicker of something pass over his face. Disappointment, maybe? "Do *you* want to get married in a church?"

He gave a shrug. "It doesn't matter."

"Do you want the boys to be there?"

"I think they should be. Also, I called Carla Sumpter and she said she can meet with us around six on Friday, if that's okay with you."

"That's fine. I have surgery in the morning and appointments until four. I should be free by then. Will our getting married prolong the adoption?"

"Let's not jump ahead of ourselves. We'll see what she has to say."

"I don't want to jeopardize your adoption of Manuel. We can always wait, or—"

"Getting cold feet already?" he asked with a penetrating assessment.

"No, but—"

"No *buts,* Raina. Manuel's going to be *our* son. And our baby is going to know both parents, however we have to do this."

However we have to do this. He was marrying her for their baby's sake, and she'd better remember that.

"You said you wanted a prenuptial agreement?"

"I think we both need one, don't you? There was a lot of information in the news about the Victims' Compensation Fund and the settlement. You need to protect what you have."

"I don't have much to protect. I used some for med school—what my scholarships didn't cover. But the rest, and any donations that came in, I gave away."

"You gave them away?" he repeated, looking shocked.

"I set up a grant program for fire companies that are affected by disasters."

"You are full of surprises," Shep said with admiration.

"I did what was right for me. And with the prenuptial agreement..." She'd considered it since he'd mentioned it, and made a decision. "Why don't we have our lawyers just draw up papers saying we take out of the marriage whatever we brought into it? That way it won't be complicated."

"I'm a wealthy man, Raina. I will definitely provide for our child and his or her future. Some should be yours if things don't work out. We're both going into this with the best of intentions, but you never know."

Suddenly she needed to get his doubts on the table. "You think I'm going to leave, don't you?"

He was silent.

"Shep, tell me why you can't believe I'll be as committed to this marriage as *you?*"

"Let's just say, history has been a forceful teacher."

"Were you involved in a serious relationship and got hurt?"

"You don't really want to hear about my past love life," he said, teasing, trying to make light of what she wanted to find out.

She met his gaze. "Yes, I do."

For a few ticking moments he was silent, staring straight ahead. When he spoke, his voice was tight. "There was a woman in California. It turned out we didn't want the same kind of life."

It was obvious he'd felt betrayed, and she wanted to know more. But she sensed Shep's protective walls wouldn't let him say more.

He was still holding her hand, and now he turned it palm up and rubbed his thumb over the center. "You're not like any woman I've ever met, and that's a good thing. I want to believe that you'll stay. But as I said, neither of us knows what will happen next." Then he smiled. "Except that you're going to have a baby—and he or she will belong to both of us."

"There's something else we need to do. Maybe

tomorrow evening we could meet with my mother and brother and tell them we're getting married."

"Are you sure you don't want to tell them without me first?"

"I've already told Ryder I'm pregnant, so he knows we're involved. Mom doesn't know anything yet."

"What did your brother say?"

"He's always on my side, no matter what happens, but he's protective. He's an older brother, so I'm not sure how he'll react to the idea of me marrying you this quickly. But that's the whole point, Shep. We *are* getting married, and I'd like to tell them together."

"If that's what you want, then that's what we'll do."

When she gazed into Shep's eyes, she saw determination and humor and desire. But if she looked deeper, she could see he'd been through a lot in his life. Telling her family they were getting married wouldn't be difficult for him. Would he eventually confide in her about his life up until the present?

In a flash of insight, she suddenly realized why facing her family wouldn't faze him. "You're willing to go through all this to be a father," she said softly.

"Yes."

Shep was a man of few words. Would he become more open with her as their relationship deepened? That was her hope.

"You're taking on a lot more than I am." He turned toward her, his thigh lodging against hers, his voice going a little husky. "Joey and Roy can be a passel of trouble, and at two, Manuel's growing into his independent stage. He says 'no' to me now," Shep added with a half smile. Showing he was thinking about their future, he continued, "I think we should build a guest cottage where Eva can stay. If you want to go back to work, maybe we can find some additional help."

Was he trying to convince her that her decision to marry him had been the right one? "Shep, moms handle three or four kids all the time."

"Not suddenly, like this. I don't want you to feel you've taken on more than you can handle."

"I'm a do-it-yourself kind of person, just as you are. Someone else helping is fine, but I think we'll want to raise our own kids. I've wanted children for a long time. The idea of taking on all of them *is* daunting, but I feel I'm ready for it. I want to be a mom just as much as you want to be a dad."

The warmth in Shep's eyes slowly turned to desire. He slipped one hand under her hair as if he relished the silky feel of it. Then he tilted her head up until her lips were very close to his. A warm breeze blew through the living room window, bringing with it the scents of overgrown fields and night dampness that was primal and filled with earthy secrets. Then there was the masculine scent of Shep, the cotton of his shirt, a trace of cologne, male pheromones. Her response to him was quick and without thought, as it always was. She twined her arms around his neck and gave herself up to the wishes that were awakening in her heart.

She'd been lost in his kiss for a few seconds…for a few minutes, when she realized Shep was pulling away. *He* had kissed *her*—but then his enthusiasm had seemed to wane. Or was it simply his restraint taking over? She felt foolish, giving in to hormones. The children were upstairs.

She was rushing headlong into this marriage because she wanted to be a mom. She wanted to protect her rights to her child, wanted a connection to a life partner that she'd missed since Clark had died. She'd fallen for Shep's strong and determined approach to life, his humor, his desire.

But had this kiss been an indication of what was going to happen in their marriage? That he'd always keep himself guarded and restrained with her? Did he want her as much as he wanted their baby?

The sobering thought had her sliding her fingers from his hair and drawing her arms to her sides.

He caught the change. "We can't expect too much," he said, leaning back against the sofa, still keeping his gaze on hers. "We have to take this slow and just see what comes."

"Are you afraid?" she asked.

"No. Just concerned that everything will work out the way we want it to."

"You mean that we'll have a good marriage?"

He nodded.

"You've never been married. I have. It does take work."

"I've never been afraid of work," he replied with a shrug and a smile. That smile made her heart flutter again, and her stomach twitter. He was one sexy cowboy.

And she was going to have to do one heck of a job selling this marriage to her family.

"This Victorian is at least a hundred years old," Shep told Raina as he walked the rooms the next morning, examining it with a builder's eye. "The way it's built, it will be here at least a hundred more."

Raina had told him they would meet her family at the Victorian, rather than at her brother's place or her mother's. She felt neutral territory was best. But Shep wasn't so sure. He'd suggested the ranch, where they could introduce the family to the boys. But Raina had wanted to go slower than that.

Shep wandered back into the kitchen where Raina was preparing iced tea.

"Be right back," she said, slipping outside onto the patio.

Trying to settle his nerves, he lifted the dessert dishes from the counter to the table and set out the napkins and silverware.

Raina returned with a smile and a handful of fresh-scented leaves. "Fresh mint." She took a sprig and held it up to his nose.

He sniffed. "That's mint, all right."

She laughed at his expression. "You're wondering why I bother. I just love the smell of mint when I'm sitting out on the patio. And it's just perfect dropped into a glass of iced tea. Will I be able to have an herb garden at the ranch?"

His large hand went around her smaller one before she could take the leaf away. "An herb garden would be nice." He took a bite of the mint leaf. "Definitely fresh."

After she took a bite, he lifted her chin. "Now let's see if we taste like mint."

He knew her mother and brother would be there any minute, but that didn't matter. The desire he felt was reflected in her gaze. Remembering their last kiss, he knew how damn hard it would be to restrain himself. This time he let a little more passion give way as his tongue searched for hers, easily tasting her and inviting her to taste him.

But she pulled away all too soon. "I don't have much time to get ready," she said breathlessly.

"It looks to me as if you *are* ready."

There was one small dish of pastries, another of cookies, a hand-painted plate with wedges of cheese and fruit. "I just have to take the corn bread from the oven. Sometimes Ryder isn't into sweets. Can you make a pot of coffee? He won't be crazy about mint tea."

Shep wasn't sure how *he'd* feel about mint tea, but he wasn't about to say so. This was Raina's evening, and he was letting her take it as far as she wanted to.

He told himself he was prepared for anything. "Is your brother going to want to throw my butt in jail for getting you pregnant?" He wasn't nervous about it, but he just didn't want to start out with her brother angry at him. Since she was close to him, Shep didn't want to interfere with that.

"Ryder's a reasonable man."

"You're saying the words, but I don't see it in your eyes."

Suddenly they heard the front door open, and Angie came hurrying in. After greeting them, she assured them, "I won't interrupt. I'll slide out the back if your mom comes in the front. I just need my laptop."

"Work?" Raina asked.

"No, Gina's wedding. All my notes are on my computer. We're going over the checklist. With the big day only a little over two weeks away, she and Logan are finally going to decide what they're doing about a honeymoon."

Raina explained, "Angie's sister Gina used to live here, too. She's marrying Logan Barnes."

"He has a son, Daniel, doesn't he?" Shep remarked.

"Do you know Logan?" Angie asked.

"He ordered supplies from us for the day-care center he built at his factory. I supervised the delivery of a lot of it and he and I got to talking. Daniel and Manuel are close together in age, so we thought they might like to play together sometime."

"That would be wonderful," Angie said enthusiastically. "We'll have to have a barbecue and invite them over. Maybe Tessa and Vince and their kids, too. Do you know Tessa Rossi, the pediatrician?"

"Yes, my boys go to her."

"Tessa used to live here, too," Raina remarked. "And one of her housemates, Emily Madison, is a midwife who works with my obstetrician. He's her husband. I'd like Emily to deliver my...our baby."

"Midwife?" Shep's chest suddenly got tight. "You're not thinking of having the baby at home?"

"What better place to have a baby? Now don't worry, Shep. You and Emily can have a nice long talk and she'll explain how safe it is, how much better for me and the baby."

Angie leaned close to Raina and whispered, "Don't spook him before the wedding."

Raina grinned at her friend. "He needs to know what he's getting into."

Raina's gaze found Shep's, and he knew she was as uncertain as he was about this marriage. Yet, he was determined to take responsibility for his child. He was also determined to look after her—and knew having her under his roof was the easiest way to do it.

Just look after her? the voice in his heart asked, the voice that kept him honest.

All right. He wanted her in his bed every night. He wanted to wake up to her face each morning. He wanted to watch her play with the kids.

Maybe he wanted too much.

When the doorbell rang a few minutes later, Angie hurried out the back, while Shep considered the best way to deal with a mom who would be concerned about her daughter's welfare and a cop who might look on him as the enemy.

A few minutes later, in the quaint but comfortable atmosphere of the Victorian's living room, Shep found himself offering his hand to first Raina's mother, Sonya Greystone, and then her brother. "I'm Shep McGraw," he said to the gray-haired woman who wore her hair in a sleek, chin-length cut. She had finer features than Raina, but he couldn't miss the resemblance.

Her brown gaze studied him quizzically, as if she wasn't quite sure why she was here. "It's nice to meet you, Mr. McGraw."

"It's Shep," he said with as friendly a smile as he could muster. He wasn't sure what Raina had told her family, but he could see they were unprepared for the news they were about to receive.

On his part, Ryder gripped Shep's hand hard, and the two men sized each other up quickly. Shep innately understood that Ryder Greystone would protect his sister at all costs.

After introductions and an uncomfortable moment, Ryder tossed out a conversational gambit. "I heard you turned the lumberyard around in a short amount of time and took on a few more men."

"When business is good, I can keep a stronger workforce."

"How can business be so good, with home construction down in this area?"

Shep could see Raina's eyes were already shooting daggers at her brother. But he could hold his own. More than his own.

"True, but home repairs are up," he replied to Ryder. "I have a couple of contractors who specialize in additions, and they like my products. Plus we're even trucking to outlying Lubbock areas. My suppliers are faster than some others. I can go on with other ways we've revved up business, but I'd probably bore you."

Raina motioned toward the kitchen. "Let's sit down. I have coffee, iced tea and snacks."

Shep's hand naturally settled at the small of Raina's back as they moved into the kitchen. He was aware that both Raina's mother and brother seemed to take note of the gesture. He waited for Raina to be seated first, and then he took the chair across from her brother.

"Raina tells me you have three boys, Mr. McGraw," Raina's mother said.

"Please call me Shep," he reminded her with a smile. "And yes, I do. Roy is six, Joey is eight and Manuel is two."

"Yes, she mentioned you have a toddler. He must keep you stepping."

"They all do."

"Do you have family in the area to help you with the children?" Mrs. Greystone asked.

"I have a housekeeper. She's good with them, as Raina can tell you." Raina was being awfully quiet, and that concerned him a little.

"I see," Sonya murmured. "You said you wanted me to meet Shep," she said to her daughter. "Are the two of you dating?"

Raina sat up straighter and met her mother's gaze. "We're not just dating, Mom. We're going to get married. That's why I invited you here. We wanted to tell you together."

Sonya pushed back her chair and stood, as if the words propelled her up. "Married? You aren't serious?"

Ryder looked from one of them to the other. "I think they're very serious, Mom."

"But how can this be? You didn't even tell me you'd met someone."

"I'm telling you now," Raina said calmly. "I also have something else to tell you. I'm pregnant."

At that, her mother seemed absolutely thunderstruck. The silence in the room was suffocating.

Shep took Raina's hand, not only to give her comfort, but to show her family they were a solid unit. "Mrs. Greystone, I know this news is surprising to you. But I want you to know I'll take good care of Raina and our baby."

"Have you ever been married?" Ryder asked.

"No, I haven't."

"Are you getting married because of the pregnancy?"

"Ryder, I don't think that's your concern," Raina answered.

"He's trying to make sure you're going to be happy." Shep could feel the tension in her hand, and he wished he could make this easier for her.

He addressed her brother. "I care about your sister and what happens to our child."

"Will you sit down, Mom?" asked Raina. "Let's talk."

The older woman sank down into her chair. "All right. But I don't think talking will change anything. You two have obviously made up your minds." She looked directly at her daughter. "I thought you might not marry again…after the way Clark died. I couldn't marry again after your father died."

"I know you couldn't. And I know you still love him. Just as a part of me will always love Clark."

"Just because you're pregnant doesn't mean you have to get married," Ryder advised his sister.

Anger flared in Raina's eyes. "Don't question my decisions, Ryder. I don't question yours."

"Maybe that's because mine are a little more well thought out."

Shep squeezed Raina's shoulder. "I think your family needs to let our news sink in."

Sonya still looked a little stunned. "Have you started planning a wedding?"

"We're going to get married in the gazebo at the courthouse," Raina replied quickly. "Probably in about a week. I want you to be there. You will come, won't you?"

"To the courthouse? Not a church?" Her mother seemed appalled by the idea.

Raina slipped away from Shep and went to her mother, crouching down beside her. "Mom, I'm pregnant and Shep's involved in an adoption. Our marriage will probably delay his adoption of Manuel. I need to go through interviews, and we'll have more home visits. We'd like to keep that process moving. Getting married quickly is the best way to do this."

"If you and your mom and brother would like to talk," Shep offered, "I can step outside." He didn't want to come between Raina and her family, yet he had *his* family to protect, too.

Raina shook her head. "No, you don't have to leave."

Raina's brother looked stern as he stood. "I think we should go. As you said, we need to absorb your news. Mom, what do you think?"

Sonya Greystone's gaze swung from Raina to Ryder. "Maybe that would be best. Raina, it's not that I don't wish you happiness. I do. But this is so sudden."

"I know, Mom."

Shep didn't like Raina's family leaving this way, but he couldn't see what he could do to make things any better right now. Hopefully, in time, both her mother and brother would realize he was going to be good to her, and to the baby she was carrying.

"Could that have been any more uncomfortable?" Raina asked with exasperation as she and Shep stood in the foyer, hearing Ryder's SUV pull away.

He rested his hand on her shoulder, wondering if her family had stirred up a hornet's nest of doubts. "You can still change your mind."

She was quiet for what seemed to be an exceptionally long moment. Finally, she replied, "I don't want to change your mind. Do you?"

After a look into her vibrant, dark eyes, he shook his head. "No, I don't. But if you need more time so your family's with you on this, I'll understand."

"I can't base my decisions on my family."

"Your circumstances are a little different than most. I can understand your mother's concerns."

"Oh, Shep. I've been alone for nine years! I want

a family. My mother can't expect me to live my life like hers."

"And your brother?"

"My brother will just have to get over himself. Where he's concerned, no one will ever be good enough for me after Clark."

With a gentle nudge, Shep tipped up her chin. "And what about the wedding? Are you sure you don't want to have it in your church? Your mother seems to think that's important."

Raina shook her head. "A judge will be fine."

He couldn't wait to bring Raina into his life. Yet something about her impatience to get married bothered him. Did she not want to get married in a church because she and Clark had been married in a church?

He remembered what her friend Angie had advised. *Just leave whatever you don't move here, then if things don't work out, you'll have a place to come home to.*

He knew he had to trust Raina if he wanted this marriage to work. He knew he had to forget Belinda and the fact that she hadn't wanted to share his life…just his bank account.

Bending to Raina, he kissed her. Chemistry took over, quickly arousing him. Raina's response was sat-isfyingly fervent. A low fire always burned between them, ready to burst into flames.

They had that. But would it be enough?

Chapter Eight

The day of their wedding, Shep straightened his bolo tie and couldn't keep a grin from his face. Alone in his bedroom—he heard Eva corralling the boys downstairs—he thought about tonight. Raina would be his wife, under his roof, and if he was lucky…in his bed. This morning he felt like the luckiest man in the world.

He had to call Cruz. He had to tell his best friend on the planet he was getting married today. Picking up his phone, he hit a speed-dial number.

"What's going on?" Cruz asked. He and Cruz didn't talk often. That wasn't their nature. But when one called the other, something important was happening.

"I'm getting married today."

He heard Cruz's sharp intake of breath. "Who?"

"Raina Gibson."

"Manuel's doctor?"

They had spoken the night before Manuel's surgery when Shep's nerves had been jangling. "So you were listening and caught her name?" Shep joked.

He knew they always listened to each other. When they'd been kids under the Willets' "care," they'd only had each other. The Willets had invited them in when Cruz was eleven and Shep was thirteen. Shep had already had enough of foster homes and folks who didn't want to adopt an "older" child. He'd admit he'd become rebellious at the Willets', uncommunicative and defiant of authority, just waiting for the day he could be on his own.

He'd stood up to Bob Willet more than once when the man was drunk and angry in order to protect himself and Cruz. They'd made a pact to bide their time until Shep was eighteen and could try to spring Cruz from the system. They'd been naive. But they'd been like brothers then and still were now.

"I more than listen," Cruz assured him. "I heard something in your voice whenever you mentioned her name. What's the story?"

"She's pregnant."

This time Cruz remained silent.

"I know. It was stupid on both our parts. But that day— Hell, neither of us were thinking."

"Obviously," Cruz remarked drily. Then he asked, "Do you *want* to get married?"

"I do." He realized those were the words he'd be using later this morning. "She's great with the boys. And…she's different, Cruz. This isn't about money or what I can give her. It's about family and making one of our own."

"Why didn't you call sooner so I could fly out?"

"We made the arrangements quickly. And I know this is a bad time for you to get away from the ranch." After the night Shep had spent in jail, he'd been angrier than he'd ever been at authority in the form of the chief of police of Sandy Cove. So in the morning when a big man with a deep voice had shown up and invited Shep to come to his ranch—he'd be taking Cruz there, too—Shep had agreed. Anything was better than the Willets' or jail. That day had changed both his and Cruz's lives.

Matt Forester lived a couple of hours north of Sandy Cove. Shep had never known exactly how Matt had heard about his situation and Cruz's. But it hadn't mattered. After months of testing Matt, seeing if he was like all the others, Shep and Cruz had realized he was a kind man who wanted the best for them both. Matt had saved their young lives and given them a real home.

"I could get away if you wanted me to," Cruz offered.

"Maybe later this year when things are more settled."

Cruz wised up to that excuse right away. "You haven't told your wife-to-be about the foster homes and jail and Matt taking us in, have you?"

"No. Her husband was a hero, Cruz, a fireman who died on September eleventh. How would she feel if she knew I almost had a record?"

"She'd understand if she cares about you."

"I'm not so sure about that. Women want their knights to be spotless. I'm not."

"You don't trust her, do you? You still don't trust that a woman will stay. Every woman isn't your mom. Every woman isn't Belinda."

"I know."

"You *don't* know. But if you're making the leap into marriage, something must have changed."

"Raina *is* different," he repeated, maybe to reassure himself. "We just haven't known each other for long."

"But you're getting married anyway. For the boys."

"And for our baby. He or she will have two parents, brothers and a good home."

"I hope you know what you're doing."

"I do."

"Then congratulations."

After Shep closed his phone, he thought about everything Cruz had said. He thought about his troubled teenage years and the people who'd turned their backs on him.

He'd *always* be there for his kids. Today Raina would promise to be there, too.

His gut told him she really did know how to keep a promise. He hoped to heaven his gut was right.

Raina stepped into the white gazebo on the front lawn of the Lubbock courthouse, her hands clammy in spite of the warm, early October day. Handsome in his dark suit, Shep held out his hand to her, looking sober, but the boyish gleam in his eyes chased away some of her nerves. She took his hand, holding on to her bouquet with the other, and together they stepped forward and stood before the judge.

The enormity of what they were doing solemnly overtook her. Yet, as she felt the presence of her mother and brother, of Lily, Gina and Logan Barnes and Angie, of Shep's boys and Eva holding little Manuel behind them, she decided once more she was doing the right thing.

Roy suddenly called out, "Hey, Dad, are you gonna say 'I do'?"

Raina laughed as she looked over her shoulder at the brothers.

Joey jabbed Roy in the ribs, giving him a scowl, but Shep answered, "You bet I am."

A second later, Shep's gaze collided with hers, and there was something in his blue eyes that made her insides twitter with an excitement that had *nothing* to do with the pregnancy. She didn't know exactly what she was getting into, but this was going to be an adventure of a lifetime.

The judge cleared his throat, ready to begin. Then he welcomed friends and family and began a ceremony that seemed to be over in the blink of an eye.

Afterward Raina remembered keeping her gaze on Shep's and saying vows. He'd done the same. She twisted the gold band on her finger and knew she'd put one on his finger, too. Yet the ceremony was somehow a foggy blur. Because she remembered much too well her wedding to Clark? Because his voice sometimes still whispered in her ears? Because so long ago sometimes seemed like yesterday?

Yet, when Shep held her in his arms, bent his head and kissed her, she was nowhere but here—in this gazebo, in front of the courthouse, kissing him. Shep's kiss was all about the two of them, and not the past. Maybe she *was* as important to him as their child. She became totally involved, totally responsive, awesomely excited, even here, even now…with a world of people watching.

Applause rang out as the kiss ended. Everyone was clapping—except for her mother and brother. What was she going to do about that? How could she convince them to support her decision?

Her mother might be easier to win over than her brother, especially if she spent any time around Shep's children. She'd have that chance in a little while. Gina had offered to host their reception on the Barnes estate. At first, Shep had refused, saying they could throw the party at the ranch. But Gina had come to both of them, convinced Shep that she and Raina were good friends and she and Logan wanted to do this for them. He'd reluctantly given in. Raina understood he didn't want to be beholden to anyone, something else she'd learned about her new husband.

Before Shep let her go, he murmured close to her ear, "You look beautiful today."

She'd chosen a Western-cut, cream lace dress with a fringed neckline and hem, and cream leather platform sandals. Along with that, she wore a Western-style hat with off-white tulle tied around it.

"Thank you," she whispered to Shep. "You look pretty good yourself." In spite of the early-afternoon heat, he wore a Western-cut suit, white shirt and bolo tie, and looked exceptionally handsome, exceptionally like a dressed-up cowboy.

"Did you bring your bathing suit like Gina suggested?" he asked. Lately the temperature had been in the eighties.

"I did, but I don't know if I'll put it on. Going swimming at a wedding reception seems a little peculiar."

"Not peculiar, just out of the ordinary. Everything we do might be a little out of the ordinary. Did you ever think of that?"

"I don't know if that makes me more afraid or more excited!"

Shep's hand slid under her hair. "I don't want you to be afraid."

She moved her cheek against his thumb. "I'll try not to be."

The judge, who seemed in a hurry to return to his chambers, shook both their hands and congratulated them. He said a few words to Ryder and then made his way back to the courthouse.

Roy asked them, "Are you married now?"

Raina dropped her arm around his shoulders. "Yes, we're married now. Are you ready for a celebration?"

"That's a party, right?" Joey asked, apparently wanting to make sure.

"Yep, it's a party with a big cake."

Raina's mother came over to her and gave her a hug. "I wish you nothing but happiness," she murmured. But when Raina pulled back, she saw her mother looked worried.

"Thank you, Mom. I think I *will* be happy, once I get used to the idea of being married again."

"It won't be the same," her mother said with a shake of her head.

"No, it won't. I don't expect it to be. Maybe that's the secret."

Shep, standing beside Raina, obviously overheard. Her mother hesitated a moment, then patted Shep's arm. "Congratulations." She smiled at Manuel and held out her hands to him. "Will you come to me?"

The two-year-old gave a wide grin, babbled and then leaned into her.

"You're a friendly one," Sonya remarked.

Roy tugged on Manuel's foot, just to tease him,

then he asked Raina's mother, "Are you going to be our grandma?"

"I guess I will be," she answered, as if she hadn't thought about that. "What do *you* think about the idea?"

"I think it's a good idea. Do you bake cookies?"

Everyone standing there laughed, and after that, conversation seemed easier. Ryder was the only one who stood apart. He and Shep just seemed to be like oil and water, and Raina didn't know if there was anything she could do about that.

They were ready to walk to their cars when Raina saw the expression on Lily's face. She asked Shep to give her a minute, and went to her friend.

Lily's eyes were moist and her lip quivered.

"I can only imagine how hard this was for you," Raina said with her arm around her friend. "If you want to skip the reception, I'll understand."

"I know you said I didn't have to come, but I wanted to. This is an important day for you, and actually, I'm glad I'm here. Hearing you and Shep say your vows reminded me of my wedding day. We didn't have very many people there either, but it was the most wonderful day of my life and I don't ever want to forget that."

"You are one strong woman," Raina said.

Lily bumped her shoulder against Raina's. "I think we're both strong women. How are *you* feeling?"

"Like I just stepped onboard a rocket ship soaring to another planet."

Lily gave her a watery smile. "That's the way a wedding is supposed to feel. Now go on, go with your groom. I'll see you at Gina's."

As soon as Raina slipped into the chauffeur-driven

limo beside Shep—he had insisted they ride in style—
he asked her, "Is Lily okay?"

"As okay as she can be. I just wish there was something more I could do to help her."

"You're helping her by being her friend." Shep's
hand covered Raina's and they sat there for a moment,
gazing straight ahead.

In the seat across from them, Roy said, "This is cool,
but everyone else is going to beat us there, Dad.
Shouldn't we go?"

"The bride and groom are supposed to arrive last,"
Shep said, joking. "We're the guests of honor."

"Us, too?" Joey asked.

"You, too. But since everyone else pulled away, I
guess it's time." He knocked on the partition between
them and the driver and nodded.

Raina heard Roy say to Joey, "I bet they're going to
hold hands all the time, now that they said 'I do'."

She wondered to herself, would they hold hands?
Would Shep be affectionate in the course of a day?
What would happen tonight when they shared the same
bed? *Would* they be sharing the same bed? In the flurry
of getting their application at the courthouse, working,
spending time with the kids, they hadn't asked or answered those questions.

But she'd be finding out some of the answers tonight.

When Raina saw what Gina had done to the pool area
of her home with Logan, tears came to her eyes. With
Shep beside her, she threw her arms around Gina and
gave her a huge hug. "Thank you so much. We never
expected anything like this."

White tables with turquoise umbrellas circled the pool. The flower arrangements on each table were the same as her bouquet—yellow roses and white gardenias. The scent of them on the breeze was heavenly. The buffet table held assorted hors d'oeuvres, crab puffs, chicken divan and prime rib for adults; pizza, chicken fingers and a crock of chili for anyone who preferred kid food.

Shep seemed a bit overwhelmed, too. He shook Logan's hand, clasped Gina's shoulder and said with heartfelt sincerity, "We'll never forget this."

"That's the idea," Gina said, teasing. "We want you indebted to us for a lifetime. That way you'll babysit Daniel whenever we need you."

Raina laughed. Gina and Logan had a wonderful nanny, Hannah, who was now rounding up the boys. After settling Manuel, along with Gina's and Logan's son, into high chairs, Raina noticed that her mother had joined Hannah and was introducing herself.

Shep bent to Raina. "Your mother's making a friend."

"She can't stay away from children. If nothing else, your boys will convince her to come out to the ranch. That is…if you want her to."

"She's your mother. Of course I want her to." He seemed disappointed in Raina that she would think differently.

"Mothers-in-law aren't always welcome. She might have suggestions."

Shep drew Raina away from the others. His hand still on her arm, he assured her, "I'll listen to whatever she has to say. That doesn't mean I'll do it. That doesn't mean *we'll* do it. But she'll be welcome, especially if she wants to give our kids attention and love."

"I'm sure I won't be able to keep her away once the baby's born. Do you think Eva will mind?"

"I think there'll be plenty for ten adults to do."

The tension that had suddenly cropped up between them dissipated. Raina realized the beginning of their marriage would seesaw like this until they were familiar with each other's quirks, sensitivities and pasts. She and Shep still had a lot to learn about each other. The question was, would he eventually be able to reveal his heart to her? She already knew each time she was with him, she was giving him a piece of hers.

"Uh-oh," she said to Shep in a low voice, watching Ryder stride toward them. "I don't like the look in his eyes."

"Easy, Raina. Give him a chance to get used to us together."

After Ryder approached the two of them, he said to Shep, "Nice reception. I imagine you could have thrown a bash like this if you'd wanted to."

Shep didn't seem to be ruffled. "Well, we couldn't refuse Gina and Logan's kind offer. Besides, Raina and I will throw a party for friends and family once she and I are more settled."

"Settled? You mean after the two of you get to know one another?"

"Ryder," Raina warned.

"Just stating the obvious," her brother said with a shrug. "This marriage was fast, and everyone knows it."

Squaring her shoulders, Raina assured him, "Everyone here does know I'm pregnant, Ryder. These are my friends."

"And where are Shep's friends?" Ryder asked.

Shep's face took on an unreadable expression, but Raina saw his jaw tighten. She took a step closer to him and laid her hand on his arm. He put his around her shoulders and she suddenly felt as if they stood as a couple against the world.

"I'm not sure why my friends are your concern," Shep said. "Besides, Raina and I decided to keep this small. There wasn't that much room around the gazebo," he remarked drily.

Ryder's eyes narrowed.

Although Shep wasn't showing it, Raina could feel the taut tension in his body. She would have to be the buffer until these two men could find some common ground. "Did you know Lily moved into the Victorian last week?"

Ryder cast a glance toward her bridesmaids. "You've really made friends since you came back to Sagebrush. I didn't know if you could fit back into small-town life."

"Once a Sagebrush girl, always a Sagebrush girl," she said, joking.

"Daddy! Daddy! Come see what we have to eat," Roy called to Shep.

"Have you met Shep's boys?" Raina asked her brother.

"No," he replied, looking over that way.

"Come on, I'll introduce you."

But before they could move away, Shep halted Ryder. "Wait."

Ryder swung around.

"Please don't tell them you're a police officer, at least not yet."

Ryder frowned. "Why shouldn't I? I'm proud of being a cop."

"I'm sure you are. But their parents were killed in an automobile accident. The police officer got to the house before the social worker did. He took them in the car to her office. Everything was handled badly."

After Ryder studied Shep for a few moments, he agreed. "Okay, I see your point." He headed toward the table where his mother was already seated with the boys.

Raina faced Shep. "I have a lot to learn about you. I didn't realize I have a lot to learn about the boys, too."

"When things come up, we'll deal with them. I don't think a crash course is going to work in a situation like this."

He was probably right. But just what would a crash course on Shep McGraw entail?

As he led her toward the kids, her stomach fluttered at the idea of finding out.

By 10:00 p.m., Roy, Joey and Manuel were all tucked in and sleeping. Raina had hugged Roy and asked Joey if it was okay to hug him, too. He'd grudgingly said yes, and she felt his hold grow a little tighter as she gave him what she hoped was the first of many bedtime comforts.

Now, however, she met Shep outside of Manuel's room. "Is he still sleeping soundly?" she asked.

"Being in the sun and dangling his toes in the pool tired him out."

After the luncheon at Gina's, many of the guests had left, including Raina's mother and brother. But Raina and Shep had changed into more casual clothes and watched the boys have fun in the pool as Logan acted as lifeguard. Raina had been super aware of Shep all afternoon. Since their glances had connected often, she suspected he'd been just as aware of her. Now, standing near his bed-room door, she felt unsure as to what to do next.

He ran his hand through his hair and shook his head. "I don't know how to play this, Raina. We got married today and should be having a honeymoon. The thing is—we're different than most married couples. I don't want to rush you into anything you don't want. I hung your clothes in my closet, but if you'd rather sleep in the guest bedroom, I'll understand."

"Do you want this to be a real marriage?" she asked, her voice a bit shaky.

He touched the back of his hand to her cheek. The feel of his taut, warm skin made her insides jump as he answered, "Hell, yes, I want this to be a real marriage."

She thought about their signed prenuptial agreement, their meeting with the caseworker and Carla Sumpter's admonition that Manuel's adoption would take longer. Now she pictured the gazebo, heard in her mind the vows she and Shep had exchanged. She considered the nine years she'd spent alone, the longing to be held again and most of all the child she was carrying.

"I want this to be a real marriage, too, starting tonight."

Shep came close enough to kiss her. Raina knew by now that he liked to start slow and ratchet up the passion. Was that a technique of his, or was that just his way with her? To her amazement, she wanted to be the only woman he thought about, the only woman who could arouse him to new heights of passion.

Touching his lips to hers, Shep reached between them and splayed his large hand over her midriff. With delib-erate slowness, he eased up her knit top, the tips of his fingers grazing her belly as he slid the material away.

His palm settled on her navel, as each of his fingers splayed across her stomach.

"It won't be long until we feel life here."

His voice was raspy, and she understood how much this baby meant to him. But what did *she* mean to him? Inside her mind, a question demanded to be asked—*Do you want me as much as this child?* But she couldn't let it out. The truth was, she was afraid of the answer.

She loved the feel of his hands protectively spread over their child, sensually spread across her skin. His cheek brushed hers as he kissed along her ear, as his tongue erotically played with her earlobe. Her knees started to buckle. She'd never felt such intense desire. Yet how could that be when she'd been married, in love with and loved by her husband for years?

That thought fled as Shep lifted her into his arms and carried her into his bedroom.

Shep set her on her feet by the bed, her arms still around his neck. He held her tightly against him. She could feel every nuance of their bodies connecting, her breasts pressed against his chest, his belt buckle against her belly, his erection pressing just where it was supposed to be.

"Do you want this as much as I do?" he asked.

The marriage—or the sex they were about to have? the devil on her shoulder demanded. Either way, at the moment, she wasn't sure it mattered. "I want it. I want *you.*"

He laughed. "Then maybe we can do it more than once. It *is* our wedding night, after all."

She suddenly worried about whether or not she could fulfill his needs.

The smile on his lips faded away. "I can tell what

you're thinking. This is about the two of us, Raina. You tell me what you want and need, and I'll tell you. We'll play, we'll explode, we'll compromise. I don't want you to do anything you don't want to do."

Right now, all she wanted was to be naked in that bed with Shep. Instead of telling him, she showed him. She slid her hands up the back of his head, nudged him down and kissed him as if it were the last kiss they'd ever share. Her boldness and desire lit the flame of his passion, and nothing went slow after that.

Shep undressed her with an abandon that she matched. After he slipped her shirt over her head and onto the floor, he unfastened her bra. Then he stood close again, letting her breasts touch his chest as he eased down her shorts. In the process, she pulled open the snaps on his shirt. Her lips at his collarbone, she kissed there and heard him groan as his palm slipped into her panties and down her backside. Each brush of his calloused fingers excited all her nerve endings. Her nipples were hard and she brushed them against his shirt. An electric spark shot from her breasts to her womb.

He shucked off his boots, jeans, briefs and shirt. She flipped her sandals to the side, and there they were, in his king-size bed, body to body, kissing, caressing, rushing toward fulfillment for both of them.

Suddenly a cry rent the air. Manuel's cry.

Shep went still and so did she.

"Bad dream?" she asked huskily.

Shep rested his jaw on top of her head. "We'll know in a second."

Another cry came. It was longer and louder. Shep didn't hesitate. He pulled away from her. "I'll be back," he mumbled hoarsely, and she knew he was still as aroused as she was. "Sometimes this can take a little while."

She could lie there waiting, or… "I'll come with you," she said, leaving the bed to find a nightgown in the closet. When he shot a questioning glance at her, she shrugged. "I'm his mother now."

Shep's slow grin was almost as arousing as a caress.

When Raina and Shep reached Manuel's room, he was standing in his crib, holding on to the rail tightly, his little face red and screwed up in a very upset expression.

When he saw Raina, he raised his arms to her.

She heard Shep grumble, "I guess a mom is more in demand than a dad this time of night."

She glanced at him over her shoulder. Bare-chested, in flannel jogging shorts with a drawstring below his navel, he looked as sexy as any man could.

"I'm a novelty," she said easily.

After a moment of considering that, Shep responded with, "I'll get him a drink of water."

After Shep left the room, she checked over Manuel. He quieted as soon as she took him in her arms, and she wondered if he'd had a bad dream. Did he remember anything of the neglect he'd experienced? Or was all of it an impression that could sometimes haunt him at night? She wanted to give him lots of love and only wonderful memories to dream about.

When Shep returned, they both held the glass as Manuel sipped.

Shep ran his thumb over the baby's forehead. "I think he had too much excitement today. He missed his nap."

Raina gave Manuel a comforting hug. He took another few sips of water and smiled at her.

After Shep took Manuel from Raina's arms, he carried him to the toy shelf and picked up a small stuffed dog. "How about this one?"

Eagerly, Manuel clutched the dog to himself and Shep settled his little boy in the crib where Manuel lay on his side clutching the dog, content once again.

"We'll see if that does it. At one of the adoption meetings, we had a session on children and sleep problems. I learned not to play with him when he wakes up like that, because then he expects it."

As Shep turned off the overhead light, leaving just the nightlight glowing, Raina saw that he tried to learn everything he could about raising his kids.

When he let her precede him through the door, she could feel his gaze on her as they returned to his bedroom. There he skimmed off his shorts and climbed into bed. Following his lead, she removed her nightgown.

His gaze followed her as she slid into bed. They were on separate sides of the bed when he asked, "Is the mood broken?"

"We'll both be listening for Manuel, to see if he's settled."

"That's not what I asked," he responded huskily.

Turning toward her husband, she suggested, "Kiss me and we'll find out."

Shep rolled toward her, reached for her, then tugged her to him. His lips came down on hers without the coaxing slowness she was used to, but at the moment, his possessive need seemed even better. She was intoxicated by his scent, tempted by his taste, excited by his arousal. As his tongue took the kiss to new heights, his hand slid between her thighs, his fingers pushed inside her and she discovered she was still aroused, still ready for him.

He tested, taunted and provoked, until she cried, "Shep, *now.*"

Moments later, Shep's body covered hers. He rose above her and spread her legs. Poised there, he slowly thrust into her, withdrew, then thrust harder. She clutched his shoulders, moaned, savored, rushed up to meet him, then unraveled with a cry that echoed in the room. Shep's body shuddered as his release followed hers.

Breathless, she held on to him, aware that this had been anything but sex for her. Somewhere between ministering to his kids and their wedding in the gazebo, she'd fallen in love with Shep McGraw. She knew he cared about their unborn child as much as he cared about his other sons. She knew that was the reason he'd married her. Hopefully, soon she'd find out if he was falling in love with *her,* too.

Chapter Nine

Standing inside Shep's walk-in closet, Raina studied her wedding dress, hanging on the rod, the fringes swinging lower than the hems on her other dresses. She couldn't help touching the tulle on the hat on the shelf above the dress, remembering everything about her wedding day…including her passionate lovemaking with Shep that night.

They'd said their vows six days ago and she still wasn't sure where she stood in their marriage. They'd made love almost every night. Yet she suspected that Shep was holding back. He gave her physical pleasure and was attentive and considerate. But she knew in her soul he wasn't risking his innermost thoughts and feelings with her. He wasn't offering her the emotional intimacy she needed in this marriage.

Yes, they talked about the practical aspects of their lives—what the boys should eat for breakfast, how much time Eva should spend with Manuel outside, if they'd go on a trail ride when they both got home from work—day-to-day things. But nothing that led to more intimate knowledge about her husband. Raina had told him so much about herself. When her mother stopped over last weekend, she'd shared even more about Raina's childhood. But Raina realized she herself was holding some things back, too—things about her marriage to Clark.

With a sigh, she took a rust-colored tunic top and tan capris from hangers and quickly dressed. She'd gotten home late tonight. Now she just wanted to change into something comfortable, talk to her husband and play with the boys. It wouldn't be too long before it was time to get them ready for bed. She wished…

She couldn't even put into words what she wished for. More time with her husband? She'd had morning sickness today and she wanted to tell Shep about it. Maybe after the boys were asleep.

Barefoot, she went into the hall and would have gone downstairs, when she heard sounds from the boys' room.

She hurried down the hall and stood at their door. When she peeked in, she could see Joey was huddled on the bed, Roy sitting beside him. Pale-gray and tiger-striped kittens who'd outgrown the barn were asleep on the corner of Roy's bed. The other two and their mama had been cavorting in the playroom when she'd passed through.

Roy spotted her immediately, and he looked as if he didn't know what to do as Joey turned his face away, wiping away tears.

Crossing to Joey's bed, she stood beside him and laid her hand gently on his shoulder. "Hey! What's going on?"

He shook his head and wouldn't look up, so she turned to Roy. Although he was younger, he was always the more vocal of the two…the one who couldn't seem to keep anything bottled up inside.

"Come on," she said, coaxing. "I want to help."

"You can't tell Dad," Joey mumbled.

"That you're upset? He'd want to know. I can't keep secrets from your father, and you shouldn't, either."

Joey scooched over to make a place for her as she sat on the bed. She wasn't going anywhere until she found out what was going on. Even if they didn't want Shep to know, they had to at least tell *her*.

After a long silence, Roy blurted out, "Ben was mean to Joey. He stole his medal, the one Dad gave him. Our first dad."

Had she and Shep missed something so important as an absent St. Christopher's medal when they'd put Joey to bed?

"When did this happen?"

"Today," Roy said without hesitation. "But Ben's been mean for a long time. That's why Joey doesn't want to go to school."

That revelation came out in a rush, as if Roy had been holding it in for a long time. Shep had told her that his phone conference with Joey's teacher had revealed nothing. Joey still dragged his feet in the mornings, but got on the school bus every day…maybe because he knew Shep expected him to.

In spite of Joey's initial resistance, Raina scooted closer to him and wrapped her arm around his shoulders.

At first she thought he might pull away. But then he gave in to all the things that were troubling him and let her hold him as he cried.

She was wiping Joey's tears from his cheek when Shep appeared in the doorway. Before he entered the room, he started to say, "Raina, if you'd like something to eat—"

He stopped when he saw the three of them huddled on the bed.

Joey tucked his head more securely into Raina's shoulder and wouldn't look at his dad.

Roy leaned over and whispered to Raina, "Joey's afraid Dad will be mad because he didn't fight Ben."

Shep's expression grew troubled. His brows drew together, and his jaw seemed more sharply angled. But his voice was calm and gentle as he asked, "What's going on?"

Bending toward Joey, Raina whispered in his ear, "I understand about Ben. But you have to look your dad in the eye and tell him what's happening at school. That's the only way he can help."

Finally, Joey lifted his head, his big dark eyes swimming with tears. Swiping them away, he sniffed, and in a low voice, told Shep, "A boy at school stole my medal and stuffed it in his desk. He's mean. In the morning before school he comes to my locker and says you don't really want us. You just took us in so we could do chores for you. He says real parents are the only parents that count."

Raina could see Joey's words disturbed Shep deeply. Anger flared in his eyes, that someone could do this to his son.

"You're mad," Roy blurted out, seeing Shep's reaction. Kids were so good at reading adults, better than parents ever imagined.

As if he were counting to ten, Shep took in a breath, let it out, then beckoned to Joey. "Come here, son."

Pulling away from the eight-year-old, Raina patted him on the back, encouraging him.

Uneasily, Joey slid off the bed and stood before Shep, looking scared and lonely and altogether unsure of what was going to happen next.

As Shep crouched down to Joey so they were on eye level, he asked, "Is this why you didn't want to go to school?"

Joey nodded.

Shep put his hand on his boy's shoulder. "Yeah, I'm angry, but not at you. I'm mad that someone didn't see this happening. I'm also angry at myself that I didn't realize what was going on. Answer me something, Joey. Do you really believe that I wanted to adopt you and Roy so you could do chores?"

Joey didn't answer right away.

The nerve in Shep's jaw pulsed, but his gaze didn't leave his son's. "Do I do chores, too?"

Biting his lower lip, Joey thought about that, then answered, "Every day. You feed the horses. You fix the fence. You ride the horses. You even mow the field sometimes."

"That's right, and when I'm not here, what do I do?"

"You go to the lumberyard. You work on the computer and carry stuff from one place to the other—stuff people build houses with."

"That's right. That's my job. Right now, you don't have a job. You have school. That's sort of where you work. Chores are always part of life. On a ranch, I guess maybe there are more than if you live in a house in town. But I believe chores teach you and Roy about work. Do you understand that?"

Joey exchanged a look with Roy, then replied, "I understand."

"Good, now I want you to listen. I adopted you because I want to be your dad. I *am* your real parent now, and I'll be your dad forever." Shep pulled Joey into a hug. "I'll fix this, Joey. We'll get your medal back." Shep straightened and tipped up his son's chin. "Believe me?"

"Yes, sir."

Shep gave him a pat on the back. "Go on, now. Get ready for bed."

"Can you read to us?" Roy asked Raina.

"Get your pj's on and brush your teeth. Pick out a good book, then I'll be back." From the look on Shep's face, he was going to do something, and she wanted to know what it was. It wouldn't be good if he acted out of anger. But she knew he was probably mad enough to do that, although he'd put that aside when he was talking to Joey. Shep seemed to be able to compartmentalize his feelings, and she didn't know if that was good or bad.

Shep nodded to Manuel's room. Knowing Eva was with the baby downstairs, Raina went to the nursery. Once she was inside, Shep shut the door. Then he paced across the small space. "Why didn't someone see what was happening to him? Why didn't *I?*"

"You can't see everything, Shep. You can't be everything."

"That's a bunch of bull, Raina. I'm supposed to see these things. He had bellyaches and Dr. Rossi suspected something might be wrong at school."

"Or at home…or because of Manuel's adoption," she added, reminding him there had been lots of possibilities.

Shep shoved his hands into his pockets. "What else did Roy and Joey tell you? What else wouldn't they tell *me?*"

Going to her husband, Raina clasped his upper arm. "They respect you, Shep. They don't want you to be disappointed in them. The stakes are a lot higher with you than they are with me."

Pushing his fingers through his hair, Shep gazed at her face, searching it, looking for the truth. "What else did they say?"

"Joey was afraid you'd think he was a coward for not fighting this…Ben. Since the incident with the medal just happened today, it might still be in his desk."

"His name's Ben Raddigan. I saw the kid at the open house before school started. He's bigger than Joey, and I think he was kept back last year. I'm going to call his parents."

This time Raina gripped Shep's arm more firmly. "Maybe you should think about notifying the teacher, and let her handle it."

"Why deal with someone who can mess this up, when I can do it myself?"

Raina wasn't sure why, but Shep seemed to have a poor opinion of authority figures. When was he going to tell her about his childhood…his teenage years? His attitude now, the way he wanted to handle this situation, was probably rooted there.

She stepped into his space until their toes were touching, until their bodies were only a few inches from contact. That seemed to get his attention. "How does Joey's teacher want you to get in touch with her if you have to?"

"I can e-mail or phone her, but Raina, you don't get—"

"I do get that you want this settled quickly, but I really believe the way not to embarrass Joey and to produce the best outcome is to consult with his teacher and see what she suggests. Some schools have a policy about this."

"About bullies?"

"Yes. It's become a real problem, and teachers are trained to deal with it. So don't take for granted that she won't listen to you and understand your concerns. She listened when you spoke with her about Joey before, didn't she?"

Their gazes collided and Raina saw the turmoil in Shep. Apparently he was torn. He wanted to do what was best for Joey but wasn't absolutely sure what that was. Finally, he nodded.

"Yes, she did. Although apparently she didn't see what was happening. I'll call her. But I'm not letting this go any longer than it has to. I'll use the phone downstairs in my office. Do you mind getting Roy and Joey ready for bed?"

She was beginning to think of herself as not only "*a* mother" but as "*their* mother." Obviously, Shep wasn't thinking of her in that way yet. She guessed he imagined that at some point, she'd really leave. But she wasn't going anywhere.

"Don't ever think I mind taking care of the boys. I feel more like a mom every day, and I think they're starting to see me that way. We're going to be parents *together,* right? They're *all* ours."

After a short silence, he nodded. "I'd like to think they are." He dropped his arm around her and brought her in for a kiss, a short but resounding kiss that lit their desire in a way that might carry into bedtime.

Desire was wonderful and exciting and thrilling, but she wanted more than desire from Shep. She loved Shep McGraw, and if he couldn't learn to love her, her heart was going to be broken once more.

In the next half hour, Raina stayed with the boys upstairs and read to them. As she turned page after page of one of their favorite books, she sensed Joey glancing at her often. Finally he asked, "What's Dad gonna do?"

Closing the book, she told him honestly, "He's speaking with your teacher. We'll figure this out, honey. I promise."

"And she keeps her promises," Roy assured his brother.

"Yes, I do."

Boots sounded on the steps. Carrying Manuel, Shep brought the toddler into Roy and Joey's room to say good night. Raina looked up at him with questioning eyes, but his expression said they'd talk after all the little cowboys were in bed. So she gave Manuel a kiss and a hug, and helped Shep tuck in Joey and Roy. Usually she hugged Joey. But tonight, *he* hugged *her.*

With the house quiet, Shep led Raina to their room, checked the baby monitor, then closed the door. "I asked Eva to come in a little earlier in the morning. Mrs. Swenson suggested I bring Joey early tomorrow. She mentioned being pleased that you sent her the note about us being married."

"I meant to tell you I did that, but it just slipped my mind."

"I guess so, with work and the kids." He hesitated a moment, then added, "And us."

Although the subject was serious, heat shot through her when he looked at her like that. "Did she listen to you?"

"Actually, she did. She didn't think it would be a good idea for me to contact Ben's parents. She'd like to handle it differently, according to the school's policies. She said they're dealing with more than bullying here… with stealing, too. And she wants to handle that between the two boys first thing in the morning. I'm not sure exactly what she's going to do. The truth is, I don't like putting this in someone else's hands. But I want to do what's best for Joey, so we'll try it her way first."

"And if her way doesn't work, you'll come out with guns blazing?" Raina guessed, half teasing, half serious.

"If that's what it takes."

She knew he meant it, and she couldn't help but wonder if he'd fight for her the same way he'd fight for his kids.

Crossing to her, he wrapped his arms around her. "You were great tonight with Joey and Roy. In fact—"

"In fact?"

"In fact, I've got to admit I was a little jealous. For over a year and a half I've been trying to get them to trust me. Tonight they trusted you as if you'd been living here and taking care of them that long, too."

"Maybe it's because I'm a woman."

"I thought about that, and maybe that's part of it. But there's more, too. Something I'm missing."

"They respect you, Shep. They love you and they don't want to let you down. Joey thought you'd be mad at him. He had a lot more to risk in telling you."

"I want them to be able to tell me anything."

She suspected the boys were hesitant to talk to him about their emotions because Shep didn't talk about his. How could she say that without it sounding like a criticism? But she didn't even know if she was right. They really hadn't been living together long enough for her to know.

"You can't fight all their battles for them, and they probably know that even better than you."

"How I handle this tomorrow is important, isn't it?"

"Yes. But loving them every day is important, too, and that's what you've been doing."

After he searched her face, seeing that she meant her words, he smiled. "You know how to make a man feel ten feet tall."

"You mean you're not that tall?" she asked, joking.

He laughed and kissed her hard, pressed his tongue into her mouth, and she felt the world drop away. Soon he was cupping her bottom and her legs were around him and she couldn't remember what they'd been talking about.

Did she want him so badly because her hormones were in turmoil from her pregnancy? Or did she want him so badly because her love for him was growing deeper each day? She didn't know. She only knew that when he kissed her like this, nothing else mattered except the joining of their bodies, their mutual pleasure and the child inside of her, who she hoped would bring them closer together.

Right now their bodies were almost as close as they could get, their clothes the only impediments. But that soon changed, as Shep's hands grabbed fistfuls of her tunic top, trying to push it out of the way. She couldn't get to his belt buckle, not as long as he was holding her this tightly.

"I can't undress you unless you put me down," she said breathlessly as he broke away to kiss her neck and then her shoulder.

"If I put you down, we'll lose momentum," he growled.

"Momentum doesn't have anywhere to go with your jeans on."

She could feel his chest ripple with his chuckle as he set her gently on her feet. By the time she'd lifted her tunic over her head and pushed off her capris, he'd shucked off his jeans and briefs. Then he was holding her again, backing her up against the closet door, kissing her as if the world was going to end tonight and he'd never get a chance to do this again.

Raina didn't know where the intensity in Shep was coming from. But she didn't care, because it set her desire ablaze in a more spectacular way than it had before. She could hardly catch her breath as he held her hands above her head and pressed tightly against her. She intertwined her fingers with his, and held on for dear life as he teased her breasts with his chest hair and his tongue searched her mouth. They'd had sex before. They'd pleasured each other before. But never with this desperate intensity and need.

He wove his fingers into her hair, stroking it away from her face, kissing her cheek and her temple, and the pulse point at the base of her throat. Shep's pleasure giving was wonderful, but she wanted it to be mutual. She ran her hands down his sides, hesitated briefly on his hips and stretched her fingers to the front of him, to the most virile part of him. When she cupped him, he bowed his forehead against hers.

"You don't play fair," he grumbled. "And because

you don't, I'm going to have to show you what teasing a man will get you."

"Bring it on," she said, challenging flirtatiously.

His gaze crashed into hers, blue eyes on brown, his filled with enough heat to melt her. Melted or not, she didn't back down, didn't close her eyes, didn't shut him out.

"You're the strongest woman I've ever met," he growled.

"And you're one of the most generous men I've ever met, opening your house to the boys…and to me."

"Opening my house to you had nothing to do with generosity." His kisses started again.

Before she thought about what he'd said, he began touching her the way a woman only dreamed of being touched. The closet door supported her as he trailed kisses to her cleavage, then made her feel like the most adored woman on earth. He kissed her breasts all over. He touched them. He caressed them. When his mouth centered on her nipple, pulling and teasing and taunting, he made her so restless she could only move against his body, expressing without words what she wanted most.

"Not yet," he whispered under his breath more than once, as her right breast became the focus of his attention this time.

Raina was trembling, her body overloading on flaming sensations. Standing here with Shep was so different than leisurely lying in bed. It seemed to enunciate more clearly each kiss and caress, each tease of his tongue on her skin, each area he'd never touched before. She was an open book to him, letting him write where he pleased. He didn't miss a line or a page.

Before she knew what he was going to attempt to do, he knelt down before her and let his palms trail over her tummy…the place where their child lay. He was always reverent about that, and it was one of the reasons she trusted him so. But then his hands clasped her hips, his thumbs tracing slow erotic circles.

She thought her blood couldn't get any hotter, but she was wrong about that. When he gently scraped his nails over her backside, then moved his thumbs into the black hair that was fine and silky, she couldn't breathe.

"Shep, we can move to the bed."

"We can do this right here."

He lowered his head, touched his tongue to her most sensitive place and she let out a little cry.

"Don't try to keep it in, Raina. If I make you feel good, I want to know."

"The boys…"

"These old walls are thick."

His tongue touched her again, left a halo of heat and began a journey he intended to finish. She could only go along for the ride. The texture of his lips was searing hot as his tongue bathed her in an iridescent storm of excitement. She arched into him. He took more of her, and then the tip of his tongue sent her to heaven. She would have collapsed into his arms, but he rose to meet her, wrapped her securely in his embrace and carried her to the bed where she turned to him, eager to love him. But he stopped her by tucking her into the crook of his arm.

"Shep, what are you doing? I want to give you pleasure, too."

"I had my pleasure watching you."

"But you're still…"

"I'll settle down when you fall asleep on my shoulder. I always do."

"But—"

"Don't overanalyze, Raina."

"If you want—"

"I'll let you know what I want and when I want it. I want you to do the same. We'll learn each other's desires. It might just take a little time."

And communication, she thought. But she also worried about tonight and what had happened. Had he pleasured her so *he* was in control? In control of what? Their sex life? What happened in their marriage? Did he even realize that, by not accepting what she wanted to give him, he was preventing them from really becoming close? Was he trying to prove to himself that he didn't need her?

Shep had so many walls that she was having a difficult time figuring them all out—and she was beginning to wonder if he would ever let her break them down.

Chapter Ten

"Is Raina going to be there?" Joey asked as Shep drove his son to school the next morning.

"No, she had appointments this morning. But I'm going to be there while you meet with Ben and your teacher. I'll be right outside the classroom door waiting, so you can tell me how it goes."

"Why can't you come in?"

"Mrs. Swenson thinks it's better if it's just her and you and Ben."

"But what if he…?"

Shep knew this was too important to say with half of his attention on the road and half of his attention on his son, so he pulled over to the shoulder. Turning to Joey, he laid his hand on his son's shoulder. "You don't know what Ben's going to say or do, but you do know what *you* can say and do."

"I don't know what to say." He looked scared.

Shep turned to look at Roy, too, who was sitting in the backseat, before he offered his advice. "I want you to both listen to me. You need to stand up for yourselves. Do you know what that means?"

"It means he should punch him," Roy mumbled.

"No, that's exactly what it *doesn't* mean. Always try to be respectful. Standing up for yourself means you tell the person who's done something wrong to you exactly how you feel."

"I'm not telling him I cried." Joey seemed horrified at the thought.

Shep almost smiled. "I can see this isn't easy. It's not easy for anybody. But you can tell him what that medal meant to you, who gave it to you, and why it's something you always want to keep. I'm not going to tell you what to say. You have to figure that out. Say the truth and what you feel. But do you understand where I'm going here?"

After staring out the windshield for a moment, Joey turned back to Shep. "So I could say something like— if he had a medal his dad gave him, he wouldn't want me to take it, would he?"

"That's right. You say the important truth that's inside here." He tapped Joey's chest.

Joey took a deep breath. "Okay, let's go."

Shep winked at Roy, put the truck in Drive, found his way into traffic again and headed for the school.

Shep's thoughts weren't just on Joey and what was about to happen to him. He couldn't stop thinking about Raina, either. He didn't know what had gotten into him last night. He seemed to want her more each time he was with her—not only want her, but claim her as his. The thing was, last night after he'd brought her to climax, he'd felt vulnerable afterward…like his soul had been ripped open and he couldn't sew it back together again. He knew he kept his guard up with everyone, except Cruz. Only the two of them understood what they'd gone through. Only the two of them knew the insecurities of being abandoned, the bravado of toughing through it, the need to succeed, the determination to wipe away everything that had gone before. Shep didn't open up with anyone else. It was too dangerous.

Yet with Raina, he found himself doing things he'd never done before, saying things he'd never said before. Marrying her had probably been an exceptionally foolish thing to do, yet she was the mother of his baby. Could she be a real mother to his sons, too? When their own child was born, would Raina be too busy for Joey and Roy and Manuel?

He didn't know.

Say the truth and tell how you feel, he'd told his son. Sometimes, as Joey would learn in the future, the truth was a little too much to tell, and protecting one's pride or heart or soul might be more important.

By the time Shep parked at the elementary school, took Roy to his classroom, then proceeded to Joey's, Joey looked less nervous and more determined. His teacher wore a serious expression and informed him Ben was already there. She'd make sure the boys were through before the other students started arriving.

"Are Ben's parents here?" Shep asked.

"No, they're not. His father said he'd stop in after school, and I hope he does."

Fifteen minutes later, Shep was pacing up and down outside the classroom, wondering why standing here waiting was harder than gentling a two-year-old colt. He'd taken off his hat and run his hand through his hair at least ten times by the time Raina came rushing up the hall. He couldn't name the feeling that filled his chest, but seeing her there felt better than making tons of money on a business deal, felt as good as a phone call from Cruz on Christmas, felt different than any feeling he'd had before. Yet the self-protective armor he'd kept in place for so many years kept his voice steady and his expression neutral.

"You came," he said simply.

She didn't look as if she knew exactly what to say, either. "I rearranged a few appointments."

Shep still felt a little caught up in what had happened last night, and he could see in her eyes that she was re-membering, too. They were newlyweds. Why should they be embarrassed by passion? But they weren't really newlyweds, were they? Not in the ordinary sense. They'd married for practicality's sake. A lifelong history of women coming and going had taught him that Raina could be gone just as quickly as she'd said "I do."

The door to the classroom suddenly opened and Joey stood there, his dark eyes big and wide as he clutched his St. Christopher medal in his hand. He rushed to Shep and said, "Mrs. Swenson made Ben clean out his desk. He still had it there. The chain's broken, but the medal's okay. Can we get a new chain?"

Shep crouched down. "Yes, we can get a new chain, a nice strong one that won't break."

"I told him what you said," Joey went on. "That he had no right to take my medal, that my dad had given it to me and he was dead and…" Joey looked up at Shep.

"It's okay," Shep said, encouraging him. "What else did you say?"

Glancing over at Raina, who'd come to stand beside him, Joey went on. "I told him that medal was supposed to keep me safe, and if there's any more trouble my new dad will take care of it."

Shep gave Joey a tight hug. "I'm real proud of you."

Joey looked up at Raina. "Will you take me to buy a chain? Dad doesn't like to shop."

With a smile only mothers could produce, she laid her hand on Joey's shoulder. "Of course I will." Then she leaned down and whispered in his ear, "I'm glad you told me. I won't make your dad go with me to the mall."

Joey laughed and glanced over his shoulder back into the classroom. "I'd better go in. The other kids will be coming soon."

As he turned to go, Raina said, "You have a good day."

Shep called, "See you later, cowboy."

Suddenly alone with Raina, Shep felt…nervous. That was crazy. He didn't get nervous around women, and he shouldn't be nervous about Raina when she was living under the same roof and sharing his bed.

What happened next really knocked him back on his heels. She turned away from him, tossed over her shoulder, "I'll be back," and took off down the hall. He would have thought she might have spotted Roy and was chasing after him, but he'd caught a glimpse of her face. It was pale, almost green.

He raced after her, stopping when he saw the word *girls* on the door. On top of that, kids started pouring in the front doors, swarming down the hall.

"Raina, are you in there? Are you okay?"

It seemed that minutes went by, though he supposed it was only seconds until her voice carried softly to him. "I'm fine. I'll be out in a minute."

That minute seemed to be a very long one, and kids looked up at him as they passed, some pointed, some giggled. He knew it was unusual for a man to be standing in front of the girls' bathroom.

Finally, when Raina came out, she didn't look much better than when she'd gone in. He took her arm, gripping her elbow. "What's going on?"

"Morning sickness. Or rather, Danish sickness. I should have known better. As long as I have a piece of toast in the morning and a little bit of juice, I'm fine. Somebody at the office had put out a tray of Danish, and my sweet tooth reared up. I don't think I even *had* a sweet tooth before I was pregnant."

He couldn't help but smile at her chagrin as they walked toward the school's entrance, then exited into the sunny October day. "Cravings are a part of pregnancy, aren't they?"

"I never believed it, but I guess they are."

Holding her arm as he was, he could feel her tremble. She looked really pale again. He was tempted to swing her up into his arms and carry her to his truck. Instead, he pointed to a bench under the shade of the building's overhang. She gratefully sank down and took a few deep breaths.

"This has happened before?" he asked.

"A few times. The first time was the day before our wedding. I thought I was just jittery. But Angie had made French toast, and I guess *that* didn't go down very well, either."

"Do you have a doctor's appointment soon?"

"In a couple of weeks."

He could suggest she go in sooner, but Raina was independent enough to make her own decisions. She wouldn't like it if he made them for her. But he was about to make one now, in spite of the consequences.

"I'm driving you to Lubbock, to your office."

"Shep, that's not necessary."

"I think it is. You're still pale and you don't seem all that steady. When I get back, I'll have Ed bring me out here to get your car."

"But I have to get home tonight."

"Give me a call when you're ready to leave, and I'll come pick you up."

"I can possibly hop a ride with Gina or Lily."

"Whatever you decide. I just don't want you taking any chances."

"I won't take chances. I'd never do anything to put this baby in harm's way. You know that, don't you?"

He studied her beautiful brown eyes and wanted to believe she was as loyal and kind and committed as she seemed. The thing was, if he believed it, he could be blindsided all the more easily.

Raina transferred the last of the chocolate macadamia nut cookies from the cookie sheet to the plate. She hoped Shep would like them.

It was almost 8:00 p.m. on Friday night and he wasn't home yet. Roy and Joey had gone to a sleepover at one of Joey's classmate's, who had a younger brother Roy's age. Shep had asked her if she minded putting Manuel to bed by herself so he could get caught up on some paperwork at the lumberyard.

No, she hadn't minded. But she did have to wonder if he didn't want to be alone with her. They hadn't made love since the night they'd both gone a little wild. He'd come to bed late the past two nights and she'd fallen asleep before he had. That bed seemed very big—and a bit lonely—when they were each on their own sides.

Two gray-and-black-striped kittens raced from under the table into the living room. She knew they'd probably end up on Roy's or Joey's bed.

Suddenly she heard the crunch of Shep's truck tires on the gravel drive. Her breath caught. She heard the engine go quiet, Shep's footfalls on the back stoop, the squeak of the screen door as he entered the kitchen, and she felt her heart race.

Settle down, she told herself. She was a married woman now, with a baby on the way. Still, her husband's smile could curl her toes.

Her husband. Was she even used to that term yet?

In the kitchen now, Shep breathed in the aroma of chocolate and butter and sugar. "Someone's been busy." He was staring at her curiously, wondering why she had baked cookies.

"Eva didn't have time today to make a treat for the weekend, so I thought I would."

He gestured to the plate she'd already fixed. "Are those for sampling?"

"Manuel's sound asleep. I thought maybe you'd like to get comfortable and go out on the front porch. It's such a beautiful night."

Through the kitchen window, they could both see the moonlit darkness stealing the last of dusk.

Shep was quiet for a while, then said, "Sure. I don't think the two of us have tried out the porch swing. We can put the baby monitor in the open window." He came closer to her, touched her turquoise earring with his forefinger, then grinned.

"Making out on a porch swing could be the perfect end to a long day."

"We can make out," she agreed. "And maybe…we can talk."

His expression changed. "Talk about…"

"I got a phone call from Mrs. Sumpter. I have an interview with a psychologist the week after next."

His focus entirely on her, he asked, "Are you worried about it?"

"Some. I just don't want anything to hold up the adoption. I know how important it is to you and Manuel."

"What are you concerned about besides that?"

"I'm worried that whoever interviews me will think we married too quickly and for the wrong reasons."

"And what will you say if he or she asks why you married me?"

It was on the tip of her tongue to blurt out "Because I love you," because that's what she'd tell the interviewer. But she didn't think Shep would accept that. It was too soon. Not only that, but a little voice in her mind whispered, *He hasn't told you what* he *feels.*

"I'll tell him or her that I want a family as much as you do, and you're a good man and I've always felt a…bond with you. We're having a baby, and I believe two parents are better than one."

"You've thought about this."

"Of course. I want to be prepared."

He wrapped his arm around her and brought her close for a kiss. Hoarsely, he said, "I'll change and be right down."

Ten minutes later they were sitting side by side on the porch swing, the dish of cookies on a table beside them accompanied by glasses of homemade lemonade. Before he'd come outside, he'd switched on the CD player in the living room. Trace Adkins sang "You're Gonna Miss This," and Raina knew it was so. Every moment was precious. Children grew up too fast and intimate moments were gone before you could catch them.

After all the passion they'd shared, Raina had thought sitting close together would seem natural. However, they both seemed off balance, and she supposed that was her fault. Shep didn't like heart-to-hearts, and that was really what she wanted to have with him.

He ate one of the chocolate cookies and offered her the plate. She shook her head.

"They're great," he said.

"Thanks."

After he finished another one, he gave her a considering look. "Morning sickness today?"

"On and off most of the day."

"Are you sure that's normal?"

"When I see Emily next week, I'll ask her."

"Are you sure about giving birth with a midwife? A hospital room with doctors around sounds better to me."

"I really believe a baby should come into the world with soft lights and lots of love surrounding him. You can be with me. The kids can even be around at the beginning of it. Emily won't take chances. If there's any problem, I'll go to the hospital and Jared Madison will take care of me."

"My stress meter will be off the charts," Shep muttered.

When the strains of the soft ballad floated through the open window, Raina suddenly stood, then held out her hand to him. "How about a dance? You can forget about your long day and the stress of my labor."

When he took her hand, the look in his eyes went from concerned to heated. Rising to his feet, he circled her with his arms. "Do you know how pretty you look tonight?"

She'd changed into a smocked, gauzy dress, the color she loved most—turquoise. She'd wanted to put on something soft and sexy, yet not too obviously so.

"When I'm away from my office, I like to look more…feminine."

He buried his nose in her hair and murmured against her ear, "You succeeded."

Instinctively, Raina wrapped her arms around Shep's neck, wanting to be as close as she possibly could to him, maybe closer than he wanted to become. Had it been a mistake to think that one day they could bare their hearts to each other completely?

With their bodies pressed together, their desire was obvious. Yet in some ways, she felt as if she had to take a step back from the physical aspect of their relationship to make the rest of it work.

The three-quarter moon cast its glow over the yard

around the porch. It was bright enough for Raina to see Shep's face as she leaned away, allowing a few inches between them.

"Tell me about your ex-fiancée," Raina requested.

Shep stilled. "Why would we want to talk about that at a time like this?"

"Because we're good in bed, Shep, but I want to feel close to you in other ways, too."

His shoulders stiffened and she thought he was going to drop his arms. But he didn't. He held her loosely. "What if I don't want to talk about her?"

She met his question head-on. "I'm not going to pull away or sulk, if that's what you think. But sometimes I still get the feeling that you think I won't stay. I just want to know more about her so it doesn't become a forbidden topic between us. I want to know *you*."

"You're in a funny mood tonight."

Maybe he was hoping she'd say "Just forget about it," but she wasn't going to do that. "How did you meet?" she asked, knowing she was prodding.

With a sigh, he answered, "On the golf course. There was a tournament for charity. She and I got paired up and it wasn't until after we broke up I found that she had asked to be my partner."

"I imagine a lot of women would have wanted to have been your partner."

"I think you're seeing it in a different way than I did. I never realized how manipulative she was. I think she was looking for someone with money to marry, and purposely went about it."

"Did *you* break off the engagement?"

"It was mutual. As soon as I started talking about returning to Texas to ranch and adopt kids, Belinda began getting cold. The day I bought Red Creek Ranch, she said goodbye. Apparently, when we got engaged she figured my money would buy fancy cars, a penthouse and servants."

"Were you living a different lifestyle in California?" She really couldn't imagine him anyplace but here.

"I had an office in Sacramento and a condo nearby. I had to wear suits a lot more often than I do now."

From his wry smile she could see he was much more comfortable with this conversation, rather than revealing his romantic past. But she wanted to know more.

"Can I ask you something without you getting angry?"

He narrowed his eyes. "Is that supposed to defuse it before it begins?"

"Maybe."

"Shoot," he replied with resignation.

"Why did you ask her to marry you?" Had he gotten engaged to *have* the family he'd never experienced?

After a silence that told her he was reluctant to reveal more, he replied, "You mean, what did I see in her that I liked? She was beautiful in a California, sun-drenched sort of way. Her parents adored her—they'd sacrificed for her education—and I thought that meant she would sacrifice for the people she loved. After all, she came from a good background."

The questions kept popping up in Raina's mind, and she didn't know how many more he'd tolerate. "How long did you date before you were engaged?"

Although his jaw tightened, he responded, "About four months. We were engaged another five months, but when I started talking about leaving California, I could see she had other plans. One night I asked if she ever wanted to have kids, and she blew up. That's when I saw a side of her she'd never shown to me before. In a temper, she said if I was thinking about moving to a hick town in Texas, I could move there alone. She would never allow her body to be changed forever by a child and she wouldn't be tied down with adopted ones, either. She wanted a lifestyle with maids and servants. She wasn't going to *be* one."

If Shep had really loved this woman, he must have been devastated. "That must have been *so* hard for you to hear."

"You could say that. I wondered how I'd been such a fool. So now do you understand why I don't like to talk about it?"

Without hesitation, she kissed him on the cheek and then laid her head on his shoulder. Shep was a private man, but he'd just revealed more than she'd ever expected.

They began swaying to the music, their bodies moving in unison once more.

This time Shep was the one to lean back. She looked up at him quizzically.

After he studied her for a verse of the song, he passed his hand down her back. "I could kiss you. I could pick you up and carry you upstairs and we could have a great time in bed. But I think all of this is coming from somewhere, and I want to know where."

With the fall of night, the air had grown cooler and she shivered. "I want us to be able to talk."

His voice was low and deep above her head. "You said that before. Why is it important?"

Now she was the one who had to be honest. "I've been thinking about my marriage to Clark."

"What kind of thinking have you been doing? Are you regretting—"

"No," she cut in. "I don't regret marrying you. I guess it's just…my marriage to Clark wasn't so perfect. Even though I was in med school, Clark really wanted us to have kids, and I did, too. I think I would have given up my career to be a mom."

Shep considered what she said. "So what happened? Why didn't you have children?"

"I couldn't get pregnant," she responded. "Med school was ferociously energy-consuming and Clark's schedule was erratic. I don't know what the problem was, but whatever it was, it was coming between us. We didn't talk about it. If there was just one thing I could change, that would be it. Whether the distance between us stemmed from my insecurities or his desire to have children, I don't know."

"It doesn't sound like you to let something like that go," Shep insisted.

"You're right. I was hoping to change things. I planned a second honeymoon, hoping that would help, but then—"

The pictures that had played over and over again on the TV screen were still so very blatant in her head. In spite of her best effort, her throat choked up and her eyes became moist as Shep held her. She let her tears fall. She wasn't sure where the sadness was coming from—from unfulfilled dreams and the loss of her husband, or from the closeness she and Clark could have had but didn't, because neither had made the effort or taken the risk.

The call of a night bird carried in the stillness as they stood on the porch, Shep stroking her back, thinking about all she'd said.

"I'm sorry," she murmured. "I don't know why I'm so…emotional. Being pregnant, I guess."

"That's not all," he decided, brushing her hair over her shoulders. "You got married a little over a week ago." Taking her face in his hands, he added, "You have a career and you're trying to be a ready-made mom. I think you should go on upstairs and get ready for bed. I'll make you a mug of hot cider and bring up some of those crackers you've been eating."

"Shep, this isn't what I intended."

"I know, but isn't our motto 'go with the flow'?" He gave her a smile that was meant to make her feel better, but it didn't. She could see the mood had been spoiled for both of them. She should have just let well enough alone. She should have settled for physical intimacy.

When Shep dropped his arms from around her, she stepped away.

Maybe talking was highly overrated. Possibly the next time, she'd just give in to the desire between them.

But was that the kind of marriage she wanted to have?

Chapter Eleven

"Enough about me," Gina said on Sunday evening, the night before her wedding. Raina, Angie and Lily had invited her over for some girl talk before the big day. "You've learned every detail I can tell you about our honeymoon plans in Kauai. It came together so much more easily, once we decided to take along Daniel and Hannah."

Although Daniel was Logan's son, Gina already thought of him as hers. Raina knew the feeling. Her heart seemed to fill to top capacity when she thought about Roy and Joey and Manuel, about the closeness she felt to them and the closeness they were beginning to feel to her. Since Joey's revelations about the bully bothering him in school, he seemed to gravitate toward her more and was much more talkative. They'd gone shopping for a chain for his medal and he'd proudly shown it to Shep.

"We'll miss you for two weeks," Angie said. She picked up the glass of sparkling apple cider sitting on the table next to her on the patio of the Victorian. "To my sister, Gina, her soon-to-be husband, Logan, and their wonderful son, Daniel. All the happiness in the world."

Sitting close together on the outside furniture, all of the women clinked their glasses and drank their cider.

With the sun teetering on the horizon in a beautiful purple-and-pink West Texas sunset, Gina turned to Lily. "If tomorrow will be too difficult for you, I'll understand. If you want to sit out the bridal party, if you want to skip the wedding altogether, just say the word."

Slowly, Lily set down her glass and met their gazes, one by one. "I don't know what I would have done the past few weeks without all of you, and that's why I want to be part of your wedding tomorrow, Gina." She settled her hand on her stomach. "Knowing Troy's baby is here makes me feel less alone." She hesitated a moment, then went on. "Something happened today and I—" She cleared her throat. "I want to tell you about it. I received a letter in the mail from Troy— from one of his friends. He'd left it with him in case anything happened."

"Oh, Lily." Raina was quick to take her friend's hand.

"It's okay," Lily replied softly. "I cried all afternoon. That's why my eyes were puffy when I came in. I couldn't help but cry. He told me how much he loved me, how much the baby and I meant to him. He also said he took a precaution before he left. He asked Mitch Cortega to look after me if anything happened."

"You and Mitch are already friends," Raina pointed out. Mitch had always been a special friend to her and

Troy, because he'd served in Iraq and had also been a member of the Texas National Guard.

"Yes, he is a friend, and he's made going back to work easier. I always told Troy I didn't need anyone to look after me, and he just laughed at that. But it *is* true. I've got to stand on my own two feet, for my sake and the baby's."

"You can stand on your own two feet and still depend on your friends," Angie insisted.

Lily smiled a little. "I guess so. But I want you to understand, I'm going to focus on the positive. I'm going to remember all the love Troy and I shared and how much he would have loved our baby. Then I'm going to give this little one the best welcome into the world he or she could ever have."

Lily addressed Gina. "So I *will* be there tomorrow, walking down the aisle ahead of you, witnessing one of the happiest days of your life." She turned her attention to Raina. "So tell us what's going on with you."

"Can I ask you a question?"

"Anything," they all chorused.

"How long does it take for a man to open up, to share what he's been through in his life, to share what he's feeling now? I don't want to compare, but Clark was very different from Shep. At the beginning of our relationship, Clark was a talker. We spent hours on the phone when we first met, talking about everything. Now I just feel…that I'm trying to open doors Shep doesn't want opened…that he's still holding back."

"Your lives are busy," Lily pointed out. "And having three kids around doesn't give you a whole lot of time to talk, does it?"

"No, I guess not."

"So, how's your sex life?" Angie asked with a straight face.

Open-mouthed for a moment, Raina finally burst out laughing. "Are you saying that's a gauge?"

"It could be an indicator," Gina agreed.

Raina remembered the night when, in some respects, their lovemaking had been hotter than it had ever been. "When we're in bed, or not even," she added mischievously, "Shep makes me feel like the most loved woman in the world. But sometimes I wonder…"

"What do you wonder?" Gina asked, gently prodding.

"If all of it isn't duty on his part. He married me because of the baby. Maybe he's just making love to me because that's what a husband is supposed to do."

"Why did *you* marry *him?*" Lily asked.

"Because I love him," she admitted out loud.

"Then give it all time," Gina advised her. "After all, it took Logan and me fourteen years to get back together. Both you and Shep are adjusting to a whole new life. Let yourself settle into it."

But just how long should Raina give their adjustment period before she should really start to worry?

Shep didn't like feeling front and center, but Gina had insisted he sit in the pew with her brother. Since he was Raina's husband, Gina now considered him family, too.

At the altar, Gina and Logan knelt for their blessing before the priest. Shep's gaze reflexively drifted toward Raina, seated in the front pew with the other bridesmaids, her beauty in the candlelight almost socking him in the gut.

This ceremony tonight had been so much different than theirs. The century-old Catholic church had a hallowedness about it that the gazebo on the courthouse lawn couldn't match. A priest had directed Gina and Logan's vows, rather than a judge.

What was wrong with him? There were good reasons why he and Raina had married as they had—Raina's pregnancy, Manuel's adoption, an urgency he'd felt as much as she had. But this church wedding had shaken him up a bit, nudged him to again think about the questions Raina had been asking. He was sure there would be more to come. She insisted that's what emotional intimacy was all about.

When in his life had he been emotionally intimate with anyone? Was he going about this marriage all wrong? But how else could he go about it, knowing that her husband had been the kind of hero that Shep didn't believe he could compete with. Not with his background.

In the pew in front of him, Gina's mother held Daniel, who was getting restless. The eighteen-month-old saw his mom and dad up at the altar and he wanted to be with them. With this wedding, Gina, Logan and Daniel would truly become a family. He and Raina and the boys were a family. What would happen when the little one was born?

Shep had to admit he couldn't wait. He just didn't want Raina to feel overwhelmed, and he'd do whatever he had to to make sure she didn't. She'd had morning sickness again today. He was afraid she was doing too much with her practice and her new responsibilities. They had a meeting tomorrow night with the adoptive parents group. He'd insisted he could go alone, but she wanted to come, too.

They were a couple.

A happily married couple?

Music began to play and Shep stood, along with everyone else, as Gina and Logan walked down the aisle, their hands intertwined as they smiled at their family and friends. Shep recognized that they shared something that he and Raina hadn't found yet.

But then he and Raina had married for a different reason than Logan and Gina—a baby.

The guests left the church pew by pew. When Shep arrived in the vestibule, his gaze cut to his wife, who stood next to Angie in the receiving line. At first his attention was caught up in the guests congratulating the newlyweds and Logan holding his son. But as his gaze drifted back to Raina and he saw her sudden pallor, he realized something was wrong. As unobtrusively as possible, he edged behind the receiving line to her side.

"What's wrong?" he murmured, close to her ear.

"I'm having cramps. They started toward the end of the ceremony. I don't want to make a scene."

"A scene be damned. Let's do what you need to do." He touched Angie's arm. "Raina's not feeling well. We're going outside."

Angie's eyes were troubled. "Should I—"

"Don't alarm Gina," Shep said. "I'll handle this. Raina will leave a message on your cell phone if we leave."

Lily, who was speaking to somebody she knew, glanced over her shoulder. Raina clutched her arm and said, "I'll see you in a bit," and left with Shep, her hand on her midriff.

"Jared already left for the reception," she told Shep as they stepped outside.

"Do you want me to call him?"

"No, I will. My cell phone's in my purse in your truck."

"Have you ever had cramping like this before?"

She shook her head.

That was all he needed. He swung her up into his arms and carried her to his vehicle. By the time he climbed into the driver's seat, she was already calling Jared.

"Jared, it's Raina. I'm cramping. What should I do?" After another pause, she responded, "Are you sure?" She looked at Shep. "He wants me to meet him at the emergency room in Lubbock."

Shep's whole body was tight with tension and his heart was doing double time. "Whatever he thinks is best. We'll be there in ten minutes."

When she closed her phone, she said, "Jared warned you to drive safely."

"As if I'm going to do anything to put this pregnancy in jeopardy," he muttered. He backed out of the parking place and headed up the main street of Sagebrush while Raina called Angie.

Ten minutes later, he parked at the emergency room lot and carried Raina inside. She didn't protest, and that told him more than anything else that *she* was scared. The fact that *she* was scared almost panicked him.

Jared must have arrived just moments before them, as he was at the registration desk already, talking to the clerk. She recognized Raina. "Dr. Gibson…McGraw. I'll do this as quickly as I can."

Shep tapped his foot, unable to define all the turmoil raging inside of him, unable to express to Raina what the thought of losing their child did to him.

The three of them made a sight, standing there in

their wedding finery. Only a half hour ago, he'd been comparing his wedding to Gina and Logan's. Only a half hour ago, the possibility of losing his child hadn't entered his mind.

Finally Jared said to Shep, "Why don't you wait out here until I examine her and do an ultrasound. I'll send someone for you when we're through."

Shep wanted to be inside there with Raina, but he didn't say so. She was sitting in a wheelchair now, looking a little lost, and he just wanted to take her into his arms and tell her everything would be okay.

"Why don't I wheel her back? I'll wait outside the exam room, but I'll be right there."

Madison looked from one of them to the other, then agreed. "Okay, follow me." Shep took hold of Raina's wheelchair and pushed it, following Madison, remembering the night he'd brought Manuel to the emergency room, the night he and Raina had really connected.

By the time Jared beckoned Shep inside the cubicle, Shep had removed his suit jacket and opened two buttons of his shirt above his bolo tie. He didn't care how he looked. He only cared what was going on in that room.

Piercing Jared Madison with his hardest stare, he asked, "How's the baby?"

"From what I can tell, everything looks fine. A few cramps and a little spotting aren't necessarily anything to be alarmed about. But pregnancies are always in a state of flux. So I'd like Raina to take a couple of days, rest, put her feet up and just give her body a chance to adjust to everything that's going on."

"Physically, you mean?"

"Emotionally, too. She's had a lot of stress."

"Good stress," Raina interjected.

"Good stress is still stress, and you know that. Fortunately, you said you have a housekeeper to take care of the boys. Right now, take advantage of that," Jared suggested.

"Can she do steps, ride in the truck?"

"What I'd like is for Raina to rest through Thursday. Can you sleep downstairs for a few nights?"

"There's a guest bedroom downstairs, where Eva sometimes stays. Raina can sleep there," Shep informed him, his chest tight with worry about Raina and their child.

"Terrific. Call my office tomorrow morning and make an appointment for Friday."

"Can I drive?" Raina asked.

"I'll drive you to the appointment," Shep cut in. "There's no use taking any chances."

Raina's voice seemed a little thick as she responded, "All right."

With a compassionate expression, Jared glanced from Raina to Shep. "I know this is scary, but what happened tonight doesn't mean there will be any trouble. Let's just take this a day at a time." He patted Raina's shoulder. "If you have any more symptoms, or if the spotting gets worse, you call me immediately."

"I will," she assured him.

At the door, Jared said, "I'll send someone back to get you checked out."

After the obstetrician left the room, complete silence enveloped it. Crossing to his wife, Shep looked down at her. "How are you doing?"

"I'm okay. How about you?"

"Shaken up. The thought of losing this baby really threw me off balance."

"Me, too," she said, but she was searching his face, looking for something.

"What?" he asked.

She shook her head. "Never mind."

He was ready to pursue the question when a nurse came in, a sheaf of papers in her hand. He knew any further talking he and Raina wanted to do would have to wait. It seemed something more was troubling her than the possibility of losing their baby.

In the car, they seemed to be locked in their separate worlds, tied up by personal thoughts. Shep didn't know how to express his worry, didn't want to add stress to a tense situation, so he kept quiet. But she was quiet, too, which was unusual for her. Maybe she was just tired. It had been a long day. Maybe her body was trying to tell her she couldn't be a doctor and a mother, too. Was she trying to reconcile that thought?

Raina's cell phone rang and she fished it out of her purse. Opening it, she answered, "Hi, Gina. You should be throwing your bouquet about now…I know you were worried, but I'm okay. I have to rest for a few days, then Jared will examine me again…Okay, put her on…Hi, Lily. No, I don't need you to come over tomorrow. It will just be me and Eva and Manuel until the boys get home…Well, sure, if you want to visit, that's fine. A laptop is only good company for so long. Okay."

Shep thought Raina was going to close the phone, but then she said, "Hi, Angie. I know. This could be nothing to worry about. I promise I'll call you if I need anything. Thank you. I'll talk to you soon. Bye."

As Raina closed her phone, Shep glanced at her. "You've got good friends."

"They all want to help."

"The problem is, they can't."

"No, they can't," she agreed. "The only thing I can do is give this time."

Shep was not going to let Raina lift a finger for the next few days.

If she lost this baby…

He wouldn't even give the thought a home in his head.

Raina walked aimlessly around the house late Saturday afternoon, stopping to stroke two of the kittens who'd curled up on the wide windowsill. After a morning of the boys roughhousing and Manuel demanding attention, Shep had decided Raina needed a break. Eva had taken Manuel along with her to her cousin's to play with her children, and Shep had taken Joey and Roy with him to run errands. Shep had been very quiet since their scare at Gina's wedding. Raina was afraid the tension between them since then had to do with an underlying question. What if she had lost the baby?

For her, Manuel and Roy and Joey had become even more precious. Yesterday Jared had given her a clean bill of health. But Shep was treating her like a piece of delicate glass, and she was worried.

Her feelings for him had grown deeper each day. She so desperately wanted him to say, "No matter what happens with your pregnancy, it's you and me against the world. I love you."

Last night she'd slept upstairs in their bedroom. Shep had held her and given her a chaste good-night kiss. When she'd asked if something was bothering him, he told her not to worry about him. She should just concentrate on taking care of herself.

She *was* taking care of herself, but she wanted to take care of *him,* too. Why wouldn't he accept that?

When the phone rang, she realized how much she missed the chatter and laughter of the boys. She lifted the phone from the dock on the end table, recognizing Ryder's number on the small screen. She hadn't told him about the miscarriage scare. She hadn't wanted a...fuss.

"Hi, there, how are you? I haven't heard from you in a while," she said brightly.

"I've been busy," he responded gruffly. "Is Shep there?"

"Not right now. He drove into town. Why?"

"Because I need to talk to you."

"So talk."

"I'd like to do this face-to-face."

"Uh-oh. I smell a problem. What's going on, Ryder?"

"I told you, I want to talk to you in person. How long will he be gone?"

"He just left about fifteen minutes ago. He was driving into Lubbock to pick up some kind of equipment. I think he might stop to get the boys new sneakers, and they'll probably convince him they need ice cream. So I imagine he'll be gone at least an hour."

"Good, I'll be over in five minutes."

"Where are you?"

"I had to stop at the police station in Sagebrush, so I'll be there almost by the time you get to the door."

"Ryder, tell me what this is about."

"It's about your husband. I'll be there in five."

Raina couldn't even imagine what Ryder had to tell her. She didn't like the fact at all that he was acting mysterious about it. Could this have anything to do with that background check he'd warned her he was going to run? It shouldn't. She'd told him to forget about it.

By the time she gathered a few toys from the sofa in the living room, she heard a rap on the kitchen screen door.

"Come in," she called, wishing Ryder felt at home here, wishing he and Shep could become friends.

Seconds later, Ryder stood in the doorway, a sober expression on his face. He was dressed in street clothes—jeans and a snap-button shirt, and he was carrying a manila envelope.

Ryder glanced around. "It's quiet. Where's the baby?"

"Eva has Manuel. Shep decided I needed a break."

Ryder crossed to the sofa where she was seated and handed her the envelope. "Do you want to read it in private, or do you want me to tell you what's in it?"

"Why don't you tell me what this is all about." She tried to remain calm. But her hands were a little clammy, and she was suddenly afraid to open the envelope.

"I told you I was going to do a background check on McGraw."

"And I told you not to."

"Yeah, well, I don't always listen to you. And it's a good thing I didn't."

"What did you find out? That he has speeding tickets?" If she kept this light, maybe nothing serious would come of it.

"I didn't just want his paper trail. I wanted real information."

"And how do you get that?"

"Old-fashioned detective work. I had a couple of road blocks, though—retirement, vacations, that kind of thing."

"I don't understand what you were investigating."

"I know cops out there, Raina. They connected me with other cops. I finally found out where McGraw spent his teenage years—in Sandy Cove, California."

"He spent his childhood in a foster home, I know that."

"More than one foster home."

"That's not unusual."

"I suppose not, but I contacted a deputy in Sandy Cove. The retired chief of police hasn't answered my calls and that made me suspicious."

"Maybe he didn't have anything to tell you."

"Possibly. But the deputy did. He remembers the night that McGraw supposedly stole a truck, though there's nothing in black and white on file."

"Supposedly?"

"McGraw was fourteen when he spent the night in jail."

"A night in jail? He was just a boy!"

"He stole a truck, Raina."

"Supposedly," she repeated. "Why doesn't the deputy know for sure?"

"He wasn't on duty that night. He just heard about what happened through the rumor mill. The chief wouldn't talk about it. The foster family kicked McGraw out, and that's *not* a 'supposedly.'"

"Where did he go?"

"Conroy, the deputy, said he was sent to stay with a guy who took in troubled kids."

Closing her eyes, Raina tried to absorb that. She hated to admit to Ryder that she knew nothing about

Shep's early years. He still hadn't opened up to her about any of that.

"I've also looked into how McGraw made his money. I haven't found anything underhanded yet, but once a hoodlum, always a hoodlum."

"People can change! Boys grow into men."

"I don't believe people change, Raina. You know that. And boys who get into trouble usually turn into men who get into trouble."

"Shep is a wonderful father," she said hotly. "You have no right—"

Ryder held up his hand to cut her off. "I'm your big brother. I have the right to protect you. Do you know anything about Shep McGraw before he moved here?"

All she knew was that a woman had hurt him deeply. She wasn't about to tell Ryder about that. "I know some things."

"The bare minimum, I bet," Ryder muttered. "I just want you to be careful. I'm going to dig around some more. If I were you, I'd do the same—quietly—without letting him know about it."

"Ryder!"

Ignoring her scolding tone, he stood and handed her the envelope. "I can see I'm not going to get very far with you. These are my notes on everyone I talked to. I intend to reach that chief of police, whether he wants to talk to me or not. After I do, I'll be in touch."

She handed him back the envelope. "I don't want this."

He settled it on her lap once again. "Don't be stupid, Raina. You have a baby to protect." After he gave her shoulder a squeeze, he strode out of the house, leaving her in a world of turmoil. Ryder had just made her question everything she thought she knew about her husband. What exactly should she do now?

Shep checked the rearview mirror and saw Roy and Joey licking ice-cream cones. He had to smile, though he was definitely going to have a mess to clean up in the backseat. "Use your napkins," he warned them.

Shep's cell phone rang and he pushed a button to put the call on the truck's speaker. "Hey, Cruz. What are you up to?"

"Just checking to see if the groom is still as happy as he was the day he got married."

"Married life is good. We had a scare this week. We thought Raina might have a miscarriage, but everything seems to be okay now."

"That's great."

"You didn't just call to congratulate me again, did you?"

"You always could read me. I wanted to let you know someone has been asking questions."

"Questions about what?"

"About you. My ranch might be two hours north, but I have friends in Sandy Cove."

Just like Sagebrush, Sandy Cove was a town where gossip traveled in circles to as many people as it could find.

"What *about* me?"

"Background stuff, mostly. When you lived where, who you lived with, where you got your money."

"I see."

"Do you know who's looking into everything?" Cruz asked.

"I can make a good guess. Raina's brother's a cop.

He and I didn't take to each other too well, so I have a feeling he's fishing."

"He won't find anything."

"Not on paper. But what he finds out depends on who he talks to."

"Not many people can remember back that far."

"I hope you're right."

"I guess you haven't told Raina what happened when you were a kid?"

"I didn't see the point."

"Maybe there is one now. Maybe you should tell her before her brother does."

"Did anyone ever tell *you* you had some smarts?"

"Just a teenage rebel named Shep, who became my older brother."

"And Matt."

"Yeah, and Matt, too. We'll never be able to repay our debt to him."

"No, but we can pass along what he gave to us by helping other kids."

Shep knew they were both thinking about growing up on Matt's ranch, what they'd learned there, what they'd been given there.

Cruz interrupted his thoughts. "If you need a character reference, give me a call."

"Will do. Thanks, Cruz, for giving me a heads-up."

"Anytime."

When Shep ended the call, both Roy and Joey were still catching drips of ice cream with their tongues on their cones. But he felt as if he'd been thrust back in time. Now he had to decide when and how to tell Raina that he'd seen the inside of a jail.

Chapter Twelve

As soon as Shep kissed Raina, he knew something was wrong. She didn't respond as she usually did. Afterward, her gaze didn't meet his—and she always looked him directly in the eye.

Granted, they hadn't been very physical the past week, not with the miscarriage scare, not with wondering what would happen if they lost the baby.

"Supper will be ready in about an hour," she told him as she turned away.

Shep had encouraged Joey and Roy to go upstairs and wash the ice cream from their hands and face. No time like the present to ask, "What's wrong?"

Good at reading people, he watched Raina do something she'd never done before.

She lied to him. "Nothing's wrong." She laid her

hand on her stomach. "I have a lot to think about, that's all. Did the boys have ice cream? Should I postpone supper another half hour?"

"Yes, they had ice cream," he answered, turmoil twisting his gut. This mundane conversation was driving him crazy. But he had to go slowly. "I brought you something," he said, hoping he was wrong about all of this, hoping she wasn't lying, hoping Ryder hadn't gotten to her.

Now she did swing around to face him. "What?"

He'd dropped the catalogues on the table when he came in. Now he picked them up and presented them to her. "I stopped at that furniture store in Lubbock that we passed a couple of times. I thought you might be interested in picking out what you want for the baby."

In the silence, there was that question between them again…the one he saw in her eyes. The one that echoed in his heart. *What would have happened if we had lost the baby?*

After she took the catalogue from him and paged through it, her eyes grew moist. "Oh, Shep. I don't know when I'll be comfortable ordering furniture, after what just happened."

He clasped her shoulders. "Hey, no pressure here. I just thought you could make a wish list."

That suggestion seemed to bring even more glistening anguish to her eyes. She murmured, "We have to talk."

"About?"

After a deep, shaky breath, she glanced toward the stairs.

"I don't even know how to begin," she said in a low

voice. "Ryder stopped by. He brought me some…information. Information about you."

Shep's body was strung tight, every nerve in it firing warning signals. "Did you *ask* him to get information?"

"No! In fact, after I told him I was pregnant he wanted to, and I told him not to."

"You knew this and you didn't tell me?"

"At that point, you and I hadn't made any decisions. I just told Ryder to forget it."

"And you really thought he'd do that?"

"I don't know. I didn't think it would matter. I didn't think he'd find anything. I trusted that you were who you seemed to be."

"And who was that, Raina?" Anger was starting to build, but he held it in, kept it locked up tight.

"You're a wonderful father, a business owner, and you seem to be a good person."

"Seem to be?" He must have let something escape in his voice, because she took a step away from him.

He dropped his hands to his sides. Damn it! Didn't he have a right to be angry? Didn't he have the right to believe she'd stand by him, not believe the first rumor that came along? Hadn't they said vows and made a commitment? Was she going to use this as an excuse to walk away?

"He's trying to protect me, Shep."

"Do you feel you *need* to be protected?"

The question seemed to sway between them, until she took hold of it and answered it. "He brought me an envelope. He gave me his notes concerning the people he'd talked to in Sandy Cove."

He could already feel her withdrawal and doubts.

"And just what did they have to say?" His tone was sarcastic, but he couldn't help it.

"Shep, this isn't easy for me. Ryder just called, came over and set it all down in front of me."

"What did he say, Raina?" Shep was having a difficult time pushing away a sense of betrayal.

"He told me you'd stolen a truck when you were fourteen, got thrown in jail and got kicked out of your foster home. He said you were sent to stay with someone who took in juveniles who got into trouble."

"And who did he get this information from?"

"A deputy. Burt Conroy. Are you saying it isn't true?"

Shep always tried to speak the truth. But sometimes the circumstances around it weren't black or white. "You know what, Raina? I'm not sure it matters if it's true or not. You've known me for months. You've watched me with my boys." He saw her wince when he called them *his,* but right now, they felt like *his,* not *theirs.* "You married me, said vows, said you'd be committed for a lifetime. So I have a question for *you.* Don't you trust your own judgment, even if you don't trust me?"

"Shep…" She reached out a hand to him, but he turned away, walked to the other side of the room, ran a hand through his hair and turned to face her once more.

"You want to know the truth? The truth is, I did steal a truck and I spent the night in jail. That's the truth."

Joey and Roy's laughter drifted down from upstairs. Shep ached so bad he couldn't stand here right now and watch the family he'd wanted to put together fall apart. Raina looked as if she was shocked at his blunt statement, as if she'd expected him to deny all of it. Maybe he shouldn't have told her in just that way, but after all, that *was* the bottom line.

He had to get out of here so he could think straight, so he could put it all in perspective. So he could decide what to do next.

"Will you be okay with Joey and Roy for a while? I think I need a little breathing space."

She looked as if she were about to burst into tears, and he wanted to do something about that, but he didn't know what. He couldn't change the past. He couldn't be somebody he wasn't. He certainly couldn't be the hero her first husband was, and that was probably the crux of the whole matter. That was probably the reason his marriage was going to fall apart.

"I'll be fine," she responded, pulling herself together. Shep could see she was hurting, too.

Yet he couldn't take on her pain. He was feeling too much of his own. When he went to the door, he called over his shoulder, "You have my cell phone number in case the boys need me."

Then he walked out and let the screen door slam behind him. Anger seemed to scald the back of his throat as he tried to figure out what hurt so bad. He was halfway into town when he realized the pain centered in his heart.

"I don't know if Shep's going to come home tonight," Raina said, confiding in Lily as she stood in the upstairs bathroom using her cell phone. Roy and Joey were downstairs in the playroom, with blankets covering the furniture as they played in their make-believe cave. They'd had a quiet supper without Shep. Roy and Joey asked where he'd gone, and she told them he had business to take care of. Even *they* knew that that was unusual on a Saturday night.

"Of course he'll come home," Lily reassured her. "Where's he going to go?"

"I don't know where he is."

"Then call him."

"He said he needed some space. Lily, what have I done? I *doubted* him."

"He told you he *did* steal the truck," her friend reminded her. Lily had pulled the whole story from her when Raina had called, looking for some support.

"Yes, he said he stole a truck. But something in the way he said it—I think there's a bigger story there. I don't think Ryder has it right, and I don't think he has all the information about it. I *do* know Shep. For just that little while this afternoon, Ryder put doubts in my head. With almost losing the baby, not knowing exactly how Shep feels about me, I'm in a rocky place. But I've known Shep ever since he started bringing his boys to me. I've watched him. He's gentle and caring with them. That can't be learned. It's innate. I just can't imagine a man with his nature being a wild, uncaring teenager. I've made a mess, Lily, and I don't know if he can ever forgive me. Maybe our marriage can't survive, even *with* the baby. Shep has good reason not to trust women, and I just gave him a reason not to trust me. He's been burned, and I burned him again."

"Raina, I want you to sit down and breathe. If you get totally stressed out it won't be good for you or the baby. Now come on. This is *one* argument. One bump. You can get over a bump."

"I don't know if Shep can."

"Have a little faith, will you?"

"I love him, Lily, but I don't know if he loves me."

"Have you told him?"

"No."

"Maybe you should. Maybe he needs to know just how much you have to lose, too. Do you want me to come over?"

Lily's presence would be comforting. They understood each other so well. But Raina wanted to be here alone when Shep came home...*if* Shep came home.

"Thanks so much for offering, but I need to wait for Shep and figure out what I'm going to say to him. I have to apologize in a way he understands—"

"If he loves you, 'I'm sorry' might be enough."

If he loves you.

Raina was almost afraid to hope.

Shep had switched on the lights in the outside, fenced-in area of the lumberyard. For the past hour he'd been moving two-by-fours from the supply area to a flatbed trailer to fill an order. He thought the activity would help. But like a broken wagon wheel thumping around and around and around, he couldn't get past his disappointment in Raina, or his anger at himself for giving in to the hope that things could be different.

He'd just hauled a few more boards onto his shoulder when the cell phone in his pocket rang. Could it be Raina? Did he want to talk to her now?

Setting down the lumber, he plucked the phone from his pocket and checked the caller ID. It was not Raina's number. It was a California number, a name he hadn't seen for a very long time—not since the night he'd spent in jail. Back then he'd spotted the name painted in black block letters on the door to the police station.

He answered, preparing himself for almost anything. "McGraw here."

"Hi, Shep, it's Chief Winston from Sandy Cove. Remember me?"

"You were definitely a memorable man in my life. I never forgot that night in jail."

"And you've held it against me ever since."

Shep sighed. "No, I let it go a long time back."

"That's good to hear. I'm calling to find out why Detective Ryder Greystone keeps calling me. I'm retired now. I took a vacation for a few weeks and didn't want to be bothered. But I had five messages from Detective Greystone. It seems he wants to know all about you and the night you spent in my jail. I have to ask, Shep. Are you in trouble of some kind?"

This man had seen Shep at his worst, when he was worried sick about Cruz and rebellious about everything that had happened with the Willets. There was no reason not to tell him the truth now.

"Greystone is investigating me because I married his sister fairly quickly. She's pregnant."

After an awkward silence, the former chief of police cleared his throat. "That's personal business. What's he trying to do, break you up?"

"Could be," Shep conceded.

After another pause, the chief finally said, "Even you don't know the real truth."

"What's that supposed to mean?"

After a momentary pause, the retired lawman continued. "The truth is, I had no choice but to put you in jail that night. If I hadn't done that, we would have had to officially give you a juvenile record, and I didn't want to. I knew the situation you were in with the Willets. I knew how careless they'd been with kids before you. I even reported them, but nothing got done. *I* was the one who called Matt Forester. We grew up together and I knew he had a good heart."

Matt had had more than a good heart. He'd taught Shep and Cruz about hard work, responsibility and getting a start in life. When he'd died, he'd left Cruz and Shep the ranch. Cruz had sold off some of it to give Shep his share. That ranch had gone a long way to making them both successful adults. Shep realized now that he'd had the wrong opinion of Chief Winston all these years. He'd thought the man had reveled in his position, that he'd thrown Shep in jail because he could. But now Shep recognized how the man had protected him, not just then, but for the future.

"You'd think a man would get smarter as he got older," Shep muttered.

"Are you talking about yourself or someone else?" the chief asked, joking.

"Why didn't you tell me you and Matt Forester were friends? Why did you let me think you just wanted to…punish me? I hated you when I was in that jail that night."

"I know you did. But I also knew you were a good kid, driving Cruz to the hospital the way you did. I guess I wanted to scare you a little, to make you see that there were rules and regulations, and you couldn't always go outside of them. I think it worked, for the most part. Matt kept me up-to-date on what was going on with you. After you moved to Texas, well, I have contacts there, too. So that's why, when a detective from Lubbock is trying to get in touch with me, I'm just not too eager to call him back. But I can, if you want me to set him straight."

Shep had grown up handling his own affairs, and that was exactly what he was going to do now. "I'm going to settle this from my end. Give me a couple of days. If he calls after that, tell him whatever you'd like."

"So what about his sister? Are you going to stay married to her?"

Shep had been sorely mistaken about the chief and his intentions. Because he'd misunderstood, his mule-headedness had categorized the chief in the wrong way. Now he realized he'd been just as mule-headed about Raina. Knowing who her first husband was, Shep had felt…unworthy.

Unworthy.

Because he'd been abandoned as a child? Overlooked for adoption? Been deserted by a selfish fiancée?

Looking at everything now, he saw clearly how unworthy he'd felt of Raina's love…as if he didn't deserve to *be* loved. He'd felt he had to compete with Clark Gibson.

Of course, he couldn't. He'd been so wrong not to pour out his past to her so she could look at it and maybe understand it. He hadn't told Raina about his troubled teenage years because of sheer pride. He didn't want her to think less of him because…

Because he loved her. His walls had broken down when he'd met her and she'd slipped inside his heart.

He'd tried to protect himself from loving her, but that hadn't worked, not one bit. He thought their physical attraction was why he wanted to be close to her, spend time with her, kiss her. Oh, sure, that might have started it all. But when he felt they might lose their baby, that she as well as the baby might be in some kind of danger, he should have admitted to himself that he loved her. He loved her with all his heart. If he'd admitted that, maybe she wouldn't have doubted him.

"Staying married to her is going to become my life's ambition. But I acted like an ass today, so I have some ground to cover first."

"Keep me informed," the chief said seriously.

Shep replied, just as seriously, "I will."

Then he went to work formulating a plan.

Raina had received the call from Shep around seven-thirty. He'd said, "We have to talk. Alone. I called Eva and she's going to bring Manuel home and stay with the boys. She should be there in about ten minutes. I'll pick you up in about fifteen, okay?"

Raina's mind had been racing. Her thoughts had screamed, *Don't decide anything without me. Give me time to let me tell you I love you.* But she hadn't wanted to say it over the phone. She wanted to look into those blue eyes of his and declare it with all the feeling in her heart.

So she simply said, "I'll be ready."

So now here they were, driving down the main street of Sagebrush, her husband tall and silent and looking troubled in the driver's seat.

"Are you okay?" he asked. "I don't want anything to happen—"

"With the baby," she finished for him in a low voice, not knowing if he was going to tell her they were finished, or if there was some way they could work through this together.

"The baby is one of the things we have to talk about," he said solemnly. "I reserved a room at the bed-and-breakfast over on Alamo Road. That way we can talk as long as we need to."

Talk about how to break up their marriage? Talk about how to explain to the kids? Talk about custody agreements and visitation arrangements? *Stop!* she warned herself, before she could make herself crazy.

The bed-and-breakfast was as old as Sagebrush. It had once housed dancing girls for the saloon down the street that had now been upgraded to a sports bar. The outside was stone and timber, refurbished as the inside had been. But Raina hardly paid attention to the tin roof covering the doorway, to the brass lamp and milk-glass shades in the foyer, to the mahogany desk where the hostess stood ready to check them in. Raina almost felt like telling her they had a whole lot of baggage that she just couldn't see.

They followed her up the staircase to a room on the second floor that was set apart from the others. Once she'd left and they were alone in the room, neither of them seemed to know what to do or say.

"Shep, I need to tell you—"

He took her hand and tugged her to the love seat. "Don't. Don't say anything yet, okay? I need to tell you some things. I should have done it long before now."

"The past doesn't matter to me, Shep."

"Well, it should." He sandwiched her hand between

both of his. "My dad and I were close. I followed him around everywhere he went and wanted to do anything he did. When he died, I sure didn't understand what had happened. My mother said something about heaven, and that that's where Dad was. That made about as much sense to me at four as when she told me we couldn't live in Texas anymore, and we ended up in California. California. Heaven. Maybe they were the same place. I was a mixed-up kid, and that didn't get any better when she left me in a shopping center and didn't come back. I was six."

Raina wanted to hold him. She wanted to kiss him. She wanted to love him. But he wasn't going to let her do that yet. He had to get this all out, and the only thing she could do was listen. She squeezed his hand.

"I became one of those kids who always had to be doing something, couldn't sit still for a minute. The foster homes I fell into just wanted a kid who would listen, not ask questions and not mouth back. So I got kicked from one to another, got angrier at the system and the adults who ran it."

It was easy for Raina to see that rebellious little boy who just wanted to be loved, but didn't know how to go about getting the love he wanted.

Shep continued, "When I was thirteen, I landed at the Willets' in Sandy Cove. But this time I lucked out. They already had taken in another foster child named Cruz, who was two years younger than me. It was as if no age difference even existed. We became brothers, in part because we knew the Willets didn't care about us. So we had to care about each other. They just wanted the money we brought in. They just wanted kids to do chores so they didn't have to. They liked to party, and they often went away and left us there alone. There wasn't anything unusual about it."

"But you were just kids. Didn't anybody check up on them?"

"They knew how to put on a good front. They knew caseworkers were overburdened. They knew we wouldn't say anything, because we had been kicked around often enough."

"Tell me the rest," she requested.

Shep stared across the room at a sepia-tinted painting of an old homestead. Finally, he shifted on the love seat and looked directly into her eyes. "They left us alone one weekend. I was fourteen and Cruz was twelve. He got sick. He had a fever before they left, but the day after they were gone, it spiked up to one hundred and four. I didn't know what to do. There was no one I could call, no hospital nearby. It was ten miles down the road in the next town. So I did what I knew how to do. I hot-wired the old truck they'd left behind and drove Cruz to the emergency room. I took him inside and told him to wait his turn and I'd be back for him later. He was scared, but he knew I couldn't stay or we'd both be in big trouble. The thing was, we never counted on one of the nurses getting the license plate number as I drove away. The authorities picked me up, waited for the Willets to get home, then all hell broke loose. The Willets claimed I was a troublemaker and it wasn't the first time I'd hot-wired the truck, so the chief of police put me in jail for the night."

"You were only fourteen! How could he do such a thing?"

"For all these years I wondered the same thing. I also didn't know how a rancher named Matt Forester came to find out about me and Cruz. He came to the jail and already had Cruz with him. He picked me up and drove us to his place, a huge ranch where he ran cattle and bred horses. That's where Cruz and I grew up, learning what was really right and wrong, what was work and what was play." He smiled a little, remembering.

"Is Mr. Forester still in California?"

"No. Matt died when I was in my early twenties. I had gotten my real-estate license and was trying to make a name for myself. Cruz had gone to college with every intention of becoming a veterinarian. But then Matt died and everything changed. Cruz decided he wanted to run the ranch. Since Matt left it to both of us, he sold off part of it to give me my stake. With that money, I bought real estate of my own, and a few years later turned it over for a nice profit." He blew out a breath. "Earlier today, Cruz called me to warn me someone was asking questions about me. Then tonight the chief of police, retired now, also called me to ask me who Ryder Greystone was. Apparently, he wanted a return call, but the chief didn't know if he should. That's when I learned that Matt Forester was one of his good friends. The chief had called him and told him two boys needed a home. All these years, I held a grudge against the chief and had a problem with authority figures. But he just threw me in jail that night to prevent the Willets from pressing charges and giving me a record. He thought it would also teach me to stay on the right side of the law."

Raina felt tears come to her eyes as she thought of

Shep as that little boy who'd lost his dad and then his mom, who'd been a teenager with no one to turn to except another boy whom he'd befriended and protected.

"Shep, I love you," she said, unable to hold in her feelings any longer. "And not because of what you told me tonight. That just confirms what I already knew. You're a noble man. You'd do anything for the people you love. It's obvious how much love you have to give—to your sons…to *our* sons. I do love you, if it's not too late to tell you that. I believe in you. I believe in *us*. Ryder just surprised me and rattled me this afternoon and threw me off balance. I'm so sorry I doubted you. If you can forgive me, I promise it will never happen again. I want to spend the rest of my life with you."

Shep didn't respond right away, and that made her nervous. But then a slow smile started at the corners of his lips and spread.

He took a small box from his pocket. "I just made it to the store before it closed. I know we didn't have a real engagement. You didn't have a real courtship."

When he opened the little black box, she gasped. It was a ring—a circle of diamonds.

"This is one of those eternity rings," he explained. "I'd like to put this on your finger as a sign that no matter what happens, we'll handle whatever it is together. It's also a promise that I'll court you for the rest of our lives. We're going to tear up that prenuptial agreement, too. What's mine is yours. I love you, Raina. My pride stood in the way of my admitting it. I couldn't see the best because I often thought about the worst—you leaving. Now I want to leave the worst behind and hold on to the future with you."

She gave him her hand. Gently, he slid the ring on her finger above her wedding band. "Perfect," he said.

"Perfect," she agreed, looking up into his eyes, letting him see everything that was in her heart.

Enfolding her in his arms, he kissed her. It was one of those shining kisses that lit their passion and seared their souls. The kiss was a coming together, a recommitment, a chance to start over the right way.

When he ended it, she clung to him, so in love she couldn't speak.

Shep pulled her onto his lap and held her in his arms. "When do you want to take a real honeymoon?"

"But the boys—"

"The boys will be fine for a couple of days without us." He settled his big hand on her tummy, "Once this baby's born, we'll hardly have time to breathe. How about three days' seclusion in Santa Fe or Taos?"

"As long as I'm with you, I don't care where we go." She could feel the chuckle in his chest as he kissed her temple.

"I'm so glad you feel that way."

"I'll feel that way for the rest of our lives."

When Shep kissed her again, she knew nothing could come between them. They were one, now and forever.

Epilogue

Raina crouched down next to the sofa, one arm around Joey, one arm around Roy.

"It's dark in here," Roy whispered in her ear.

"Only for a few more minutes."

Beside her on the sofa, Angie held Manuel. The toddler reached for Raina's hair and held on to it. "Mommy," he said quite clearly.

The light over the stove in the kitchen glowed softly, some of its illumination splaying into the living room. Raina reached over Roy's shoulder and patted Manuel's face. "Hey, sweet one. I know you're there."

For the past month, she'd truly become the happiest woman to walk the planet. She felt like a mom. She knew being a mother to three kids, and soon an infant, wouldn't be easy. Yet she also knew her husband loved her as much as she loved him. That gave her all the confidence in the world that she could handle anything… with a little help.

Lily, who was standing on the other side of Joey, said in a low voice, "I think he's coming. Get ready, everyone."

Lily had been a real trouper. Raina knew how difficult the past few months had been for her, how raw her grief was, yet how unbreakable her spirit seemed to be.

The kitchen door opened and shut. Shep's strong, deep voice called, "Raina?"

When he stepped into the living room, someone switched on the overhead light and everyone popped out of their hiding places.

"Surprise!" Roy and Joey called the loudest, running toward their father.

Grinning, Shep gave both of them a big hug. "What are you surprising me with?"

"A party," Roy answered gleefully.

Raina went to her cowboy, who looked a bit overwhelmed. "Happy birthday!"

Shep looked around at everyone, obviously speechless. His gaze fell on their friends—Logan, Gina and their son Daniel, Angie and Lily, Raina's mother and Ryder. When his gaze fell on Ryder, his eyebrows arched up. Ryder approached him and held out his hand for a shake. Shep firmly shook it.

With Raina standing right there, Ryder admitted, "I've never seen my sister happier, so I brought a present you might appreciate." He handed Shep a dark blue gift bag.

"Go ahead," Raina encouraged him. "Then we'll feed everyone ice cream and cake."

Shep dipped his hand into the bag and pulled out a branch.

"It's an olive branch," Ryder said. "I thought maybe we could start over."

"I'd like that," Shep told him sincerely, then caught Raina around the waist and gave her a hug. "Did you plan this?"

"No! Honestly, Ryder thought about it all on his own."

Joey pointed to a table that had been set up in the corner. "There's more presents over there."

"I see, but I think I have the best present I'll ever get right here."

"What's that?" Roy asked.

"Your mom, your new brother or sister and the three of you. I couldn't ask for anything more."

"I have a special present for you," Raina said, her hand caressing his jaw.

"But I have to wait until everyone's gone, right?" Shep asked wickedly.

She could feel a flush stain her cheeks. Their time in the bedroom was precious and passionate with the love and commitment and promise they shared every day. "If you blow out all the candles on your cake, you might get that wish," she said, teasing. "But no, I have another surprise. Come on out," she called toward the playroom.

Cruz Martinez emerged from the playroom and Shep's mouth dropped open. He was a striking man who wore a smile that practically spread from ear to ear. He was as tall as Shep and just as lean. As he embraced her husband, the affection and caring that the two of them shared was obvious.

Finally, Shep stepped back. "So I guess the two of you have met," he said, joking.

"We're already friends," Cruz told him. "I like your new wife. She knows how to throw a party."

Shep laughed out loud and Raina could hear the true happiness in that laughter.

"I'll be right back," he said to everyone, taking Raina's hand and pulling her through the doorway into the kitchen.

"They're going to kiss," Joey announced to everyone.

"What are you doing?" Raina asked Shep. "This is your party. We have guests."

"Thank you for going to so much trouble, for giving me a gift that means so much more than you can ever know."

"I know," she said softly, wrapping her arms around his neck.

Her cowboy bent his head and kissed her.

The round of applause from the living room just made them both hold on tighter. They'd be spending a lifetime holding on tightly to each other, keeping promises and giving each other gifts they'd cherish always.

* * * * *

Don't miss the next book in Karen Rose Smith's
THE BABY EXPERTS *miniseries,*
coming in December 2010,
wherever Silhouette Books are sold.

Kay Young returned to woozy consciousness to find that she was lying on a soft sofa beneath a heap of quilts near a cheerfully burning fire. When she tried to move, however, everything hurt, and she groaned.

At once she heard a sound, then a stranger with a hard, harsh face was squatting beside her. "Shh," he said softly. "You're safe here. I promise."

"I have to go," she said weakly, struggling against pain. "He'll find me. He can't find me."

"Easy, lady," he said quietly. "You're hurt. No one's going to find you here."

"He will," she said desperately, terror clutching at her insides. "He always finds me!"

"Easy," he said again. "There's a blizzard outside. No one's getting here tonight, not even the doctor. I know, because I tried."

"Doctor? I don't need a doctor! I've got to get away."

"There's nowhere to go tonight," he said levelly. "And if I thought you could stand, I'd take you to a window and show you."

But even as she tried once more to pull away the quilts, she remembered something else: this man had been gentle when he'd found her beside the road, even when she had kicked and clawed. He hadn't hurt her.

Terror receded just a bit. She looked at him and detected signs of true concern there.

The terror eased another notch and she let her head sag on the pillow. "He always finds me," she whispered.

"Not here. Not tonight. That much I can guarantee."

Will Kay's mysterious rescuer
protect her from her worst fears?
Find out in HER HERO IN HIDING by New York
Times bestselling author Rachel Lee.
Available June 2010,
only from Silhouette® Romantic Suspense.

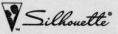

ROMANTIC
SUSPENSE

Sparked by Danger, Fueled by Passion.

NEW YORK TIMES AND *USA TODAY*
BESTSELLING AUTHOR

RACHEL LEE

BRINGS YOU AN ALL-NEW
CONARD COUNTY: THE NEXT GENERATION SAGA!

After finding the injured Kay Young on a deserted country
road Clint Ardmore learns that she is not only being hunted
by a serial killer, but is also three months pregnant.
He is determined to protect them—even if it means
forgoing the solitude that he has come to appreciate.
But will Clint grow fond of having an attractive woman
occupy his otherwise empty ranch?

Find out in

Her Hero in Hiding

Available June 2010 wherever books are sold.

Visit Silhouette Books at www.eHarlequin.com

SRS27681

The Best Man in Texas
TANYA MICHAELS

Brooke Nichols—soon to be Brooke Baker—
hates surprises. Growing up in an unstable
environment, she's happy to be putting down
roots with her safe, steady fiancé. Then she meets
his best friend, Jake McBride, a firefighter and
former soldier who's raw, unpredictable and
passionate. With his spontaneous streak and
dangerous career, Jake is everything Brooke is
trying to avoid…so why is it so hard to resist him?

**Available June
wherever books are sold.**

"LOVE, HOME & HAPPINESS"

www.eHarlequin.com

HAR75315

HARLEQUIN® Romance®

GIRLS' Weekend in VEGAS

Four friends, four dream weddings!

On a girly weekend in Las Vegas, best friends Alex, Molly,
Serena and Jayne are supposed to just have fun and forget
men, but they end up meeting their perfect matches!
Will the love they find in Vegas stay in Vegas?

Find out in this sassy, fun and wildly romantic miniseries
all about love and friendship!

Saving Cinderella! by MYRNA MACKENZIE
Available June

Vegas Pregnancy Surprise by SHIRLEY JUMP
Available July

Inconveniently Wed! by JACKIE BRAUN
Available August

Wedding Date with the Best Man
by MELISSA McCLONE
Available September

REQUEST YOUR FREE BOOKS!

2 FREE NOVELS PLUS 2 FREE GIFTS!

SPECIAL EDITION
Life, Love and Family!

YES! Please send me 2 FREE Silhouette® Special Edition® novels and my 2 FREE gifts (gifts are worth about $10). After receiving them, if I don't wish to receive any more books, I can return the shipping statement marked "cancel." If I don't cancel, I will receive 6 brand-new novels every month and be billed just $4.24 per book in the U.S. or $4.99 per book in Canada. That's a saving of 15% off the cover price! It's quite a bargain! Shipping and handling is just 50¢ per book.* I understand that accepting the 2 free books and gifts places me under no obligation to buy anything. I can always return a shipment and cancel at any time. Even if I never buy another book from Silhouette, the two free books and gifts are mine to keep forever.

235/335 SDN E5RG

Name	(PLEASE PRINT)	
Address		Apt. #
City	State/Prov.	Zip/Postal Code

Signature (if under 18, a parent or guardian must sign)

Mail to the Silhouette Reader Service:
IN U.S.A.: P.O. Box 1867, Buffalo, NY 14240-1867
IN CANADA: P.O. Box 609, Fort Erie, Ontario L2A 5X3

Not valid for current subscribers to Silhouette Special Edition books.

Want to try two free books from another line?
Call 1-800-873-8635 or visit www.morefreebooks.com.

* Terms and prices subject to change without notice. Prices do not include applicable taxes. N.Y. residents add applicable sales tax. Canadian residents will be charged applicable provincial taxes and GST. Offer not valid in Quebec. This offer is limited to one order per household. All orders subject to approval. Credit or debit balances in a customer's account(s) may be offset by any other outstanding balance owed by or to the customer. Please allow 4 to 6 weeks for delivery. Offer available while quantities last.

Your Privacy: Silhouette is committed to protecting your privacy. Our Privacy Policy is available online at www.eHarlequin.com or upon request from the Reader Service. From time to time we make our lists of customers available to reputable third parties who may have a product or service of interest to you. If you would prefer we not share your name and address, please check here. ☐

Help us get it right—We strive for accurate, respectful and relevant communications. To clarify or modify your communication preferences, visit us at www.ReaderService.com/consumerschoice.

SSE10R